The
Food Book

AMONG THE AUTHOR'S EARLIER BOOKS

The
Food Book

BRIAN J. FORD

HAMISH HAMILTON LONDON

First published in Great Britain 1986
by Hamish Hamilton Ltd
27 Wrights Lane London W8 5TZ

British Library Cataloguing in Publication Data

Ford, Brian J.
  The food book.
  1. Food   2. Health
  1. Title
  613'.2   TX353

  ISBN 0–241–11834–4

Typeset by Input Typesetting Ltd, London
Printed in Great Britain by
St Edmundsbury Press, Suffolk

INTRODUCTION

People are suffering. Not so much from additives or cholesterol, nor from over-eating; but from the burden of stress and insecurity which the Cult of the Expert is generating. Experts insist that our food is poisoning us, that our diet is a danger, or that our children are threatened by the food they eat. Experts from the other side stress, equally convincingly, that chemically-treated food does no harm to anyone, that additives are not proven hazards, and that the protesters are cranks. Our era is wrestling with opinion diversity in areas where understanding is nearer than we think. Polarisation of viewpoint is the norm. Nothing is a question of degree, of shades of grey that merge from light to dark, in the current age of polarised principle. It is true of political movements, religious sects, economic theories; everything is white or black. There are good ideas, to which proponents adhere, and all others are bad, irrefutably bad.

This view is a passing phase. It is an aberration. Societal values cannot face the future like this – we need to understand that issues often transcend the definitive clinicality of traditional science. Science is no match for these modern debates. Reality is *not* polarised; it is only the fickleness of history that finds us living through an age when we have tricked ourselves into *thinking* it is. Some processed food is admirable. Some additives are useful. Some foods are best avoided. There are 'natural' foods that are very dangerous; there are 'artificial' foods that are not. Experts who campaign to press food on us which may be rich in unnecessary additives are

1

wrong. Experts who say every additive should be avoided like the plague are also wrong. As is the case in most debatable issues, there is some right on both sides and it is the task of this book to show how opinions can be weighed and assessed. Experts enjoy waving risks at you like banners. What they do not do is present the issues so that you can best make up your own mind, for they have a vested interest in keeping the public in the dark about what is really going on. That has often been the case in the food industry, of course; but I now wish to draw attention to the same danger from the other side. Many of the arguments from the food lobby, if I can use that phrase, are muddled, erroneously expressed, sometimes simply false. Food is not the great danger. Expert opinions are the problem, and since awareness of the issues is the best ammunition to use against those who seek to blind with obscurity then the message of this book may help boost your personal immunity to the effects of stress induced by campaigners from both sides.

Experts proclaim that one-third of the population is overweight. I am more intrigued by the fact that, although virtually everyone eats the wrong kind of food, two-thirds of us are *not* overweight in spite of our gluttony. Experts proclaim that saturated animal fats are bad for us, so the diet freaks eat cheese instead. Cheese is richer in saturated animal fats than almost any other food. Experts proclaim that cholesterol is nothing but a danger. Yet your brain is built of it, and without it you would die. Experts insist that their additives are no worse than other items in our diet – but that is no argument against lowering the risks, by removing surplus additives from the food-production industry. For reasons I shall explain, the food industrialist is obsessed by additives, the modern processor is addicted to them.

People struggle round hypermarkets, jostling with each other, selecting food in plastic wrappers; then they stand in line waiting interminably for the check-out girl to attend to them; they load the food from shelf to trolley, from trolley to desk, from till to trolley, from trolley to car, from car to doorstep, from doorstep to kitchen worktop, from there to shelf . . . seven times each package is handled in the process. Why? Because people have been fooled into believing that they need to save the money. How does that square with the gadget-ridden cars in which they reach the super-market? No expense is spared in adornment of the mobile territory of the car – it is a classy Volvo estate, a snappy BMW, a solid

2

and dependable Merc which takes the successful shopper to the hypermarket. One of those didn't 'save money'. They'd have bought a rusting but reliable Cortina from the 1970s if saving money *really* mattered. So if saving money is not really the answer, why do they do it? Hypermarket shopping is merely the fashion, that is all; don't try to rationalise it. The corner shop is usually far more convenient, the local shopping centre far more civilised, than the cattle-market hypermarket can be. Oh yes, they have their uses; but do not be tricked into misconstruing your motives.

If it is not money that we are saving, it is *time*. Or so they say. But how much time does it take to prepare meals? How much family contact revolves around the arranging of mealtimes? How much discussion centres on the family table, with a meal jointly prepared which all enjoy? People who pop frozen, mushy foods into a microwave oven are saving time to collapse in front of a television set more often than not. Or they may go out and sail, or bop, or play squash . . . all energetic occupations, so where did the need to 'collapse' in front of the TV originate? Not out of tiredness at all, but out of boredom. The job has become a means of producing money, which fuels the car, the microwave, the TV licence, so one is running on a slowly contracting treadmill. The fun of making meals, the tiny time it takes to arrange a table, the lively fun that goes on at mealtimes, the sharing of experiences and the planning of a future together are all part of life as it should be in the future. Forget the drab past of Victorian values. Throw over the current vogue for disposable possessions, disposable people. Look instead at food as a great liberating experience that brings the fun into family life.

Do not believe those who try to say that people would *rather* sit in front of TV and eat out of a plastic tray. The evidence shows that to be untrue. People spend a fortune on meals in restaurants, prices that are in Britain traditionally inflated (in most other countries they are lower; in France, where the food is at its best, the cost of eating out is much less even though the cost of the raw ingredients is much more). It is equally untrue that children will only eat junk. They eat what they like. Cook vegetables properly, and children will love them. The problem with children and eating is that you teach them not to like vegetables. You pile them onto the plate, you tell them to eat it because it's good for them, you tell them they'll have no pudding until they have eaten it all. That's if you are a yesterday parent. A modern parent will give kids additive-rich frozen ready-made meals from the freezer centre and then sit mutely staring at TV whilst they munch disconsolately at the chemically flavoured and formless mass. A future parent will do none of these things. The future parent will remember how you never hear anybody say: 'Now eat all that icecream up, and until you finish it you'll sit there!' Neither do you find the expression: 'Because you have been such marvellous fun today, I'm giving you some more cabbage – but for heaven's sake do not spill it or that'll be the last you get from me!' We only use *negative* loading for things we expect the children to dislike, and the *positive* for things they ought to like. Turn the meanings round and you can see the bias of which I write. Well-cooked vegetables, boiled for just the right time in a little water, dotted with butter, decorated with a contrast of colour (a little diced ham for peas, a sprinkling of chives for carrots), and left for children to help themselves will allow them the freedom to find the foods they like, and to begin to learn that dogmatic opinions from parents are the root cause of all that polarisation of inflexibility in adult life. You are what you eat, they say, but that cannot be right. The body discards the foodstuffs it does not require, and in fact you are what you retain. It is far truer to say *you are what you learn*. Children, faced with foods they have never seen before, do not know what they like: they like what they know. And what they do know is often implanted by parental attitudes.

You can prove that easily enough if you look at the diet they choose as adults – gone are the monster-crisps, the dripping ice lollies, the glutinous burgers; in their place are the avocadoes, the broccoli, the asparagus, the fillet steak. Meanwhile, parental propaganda kept all this away from the children, and they missed out for years on all the fun. It is time we were more open about food, and made for ouselves a future where our ideas were liberated for a change.

The difficulty we have is in sorting out the sensible theories from the fads. There have been several calls for government action to compel food manufacturers to limit some foods and to institute a legal food policy, but I do not feel that is appropriate. Views change. Some years ago we might have imposed limits on carbo-hydrates, when they happened to be the trendy target for attack; currently people tend to take extra vitamins (and some of them die in consequence). Official action is an unwise answer. Public opinion and the pressure of people who know what they wish to

4

buy is a better one. The old view that we must buy what the industry provides is false – look at the amount of wholemeal bread in supermarkets, resulting from public demand.

Many of the targets for attack are chosen for questionable criteria, if only people questioned them. The current war against additives is an example. I have campaigned against their overuse for years, and have scored some minor successes in that continuing battle. But these days people tend to assume we should be against *all* additives. Many of these substances are of the greatest value, and public health would suffer if they went. What we need is a new understanding for the future which will enable us to work out the optimum answer. Polarisation of opinion is not the solution and never can be.

Wholemeal bread is a case in point. Everyone is eating it these days, for it has become a fashionable item of the daily diet. Yet bread causes disease. There may be a million people in the UK suffering because of diseases caused by bread. So it is with bran and muesli. The risks we run from a low-roughage diet have made opinion in this polarised era assume that a high-fibre diet is the answer. But too much fibre can be bad for some people. Here too the solution is to have a diet that is moderately rich in fibre, for either extreme is undesirable.

Politics come into it too. We are all enjoined to add milk to every dish you can think of, to spoil ourselves with cream, to eat more cheese; and this (in spite of what it looks like) is not a campaign designed to boost the nation's health. It is intended to get rid of the milk surplus which Europe now produces. We have to throw it all away if it is not consumed, so we trick people into taking more than they would. Many people are allergic to milk, which can make them ill. Dairy produce is rich in saturated animal fats, so it is bad on that score too. Once again we need a doctrine of moderation, and not one of extremes. And we must face the fact that many of the foods we revere for their health-giving propensities are actually often bad for us. The vogue for pulses and a diet rich in beans can expose us to serious health hazards, for example. The stand-by of celery which dieters love can pose problems under certain circumstances. And, as we shall see, tables for weight and height can lead you badly astray.

There is some nutrition explained in this book, but that is a subject which others are better fitted to examine. A little cookery creeps in too, though I am only an amateur chef. But the main

5

thrust of the argument is to inform and illustrate – to provide background facts on the biology of what we eat and why we are eating it. It is your mind that has to be made up; and for that you need access to ideas and data. Polarisation provides controversy, heated argument, dissension; insight provides the key to calm and sensible appraisal.

In particular, I have tried to throw some light on the debates over fats and sugar, diet and health. I am certain that the conventional view on dieting is wrong – we should abandon the need to control our diet in order to set a weight ordained by a textbook. The body sets its own weight. If that changes it may be for your own good. You can certainly reduce your weight if it is excessive, and there is clear evidence this is a good thing to do if your inner balance – triggered by your *adipostat* (a kind of 'thermostat' for weight) – gives you an excessive amount of weight gain. But you do not have to regulate your weight by conscious effort all the while. No species has to do that, for the mechanisms are part of our evolutionary history.

Some statistical background has crept in, but we are less certain about cause and effect than we pretend. The Cult of the Expert likes to spread the notion that the public are really rather dull, and need paternalistic propaganda from a gifted minority. Statistics are a mainstay of many arguments, and they are a hazardous minefield through which to weave a thread of truth. You can produce statistics to associate almost any food with almost any effect, even if the two are unrelated. This *parallel causality*, which is explored later on, has misled us more than once.

Most of our problem stems from a lifestyle of conformity, inactivity, impotence and restriction. A change in the way we live could probably do more to improve public health than any dietary modification. There are many exceptions to the supposed orthodoxies about sugar, saturated fats, obesity and health. But one statistic which is less widely cited is the strong correlation between death from coronary disease and watching television. Either the rays are doing the damage, or the lifestyle. I would opt for the latter. And that is why a feature of this book is a plan of personal action – some ideas how you can take control of your own decision-making, and set personal priorities.

London 1986

CHAPTER ONE

Not so long ago everyone knew that, if there was one sure way to change your dietary intake in order to lose weight and stay healthy, the first things to give up were bread and potatoes. Things are different in the eighties. Now the dietary advice is that, to keep a balanced diet, the main thing is to ensure an adequate ration of – potatoes and bread.

How can you make sense of it all? There has never been a greater emphasis on diet, health, food and fitness; but the public are more confused (and less well-informed) than ever. We must recognise that we live in an age of polarisation. People know that there are strong food lobbies, designed to propagandise a specific viewpoint and to sell a commercial product. But the proponents of the exactly opposite viewpoint are just as keen on propagandising a specific, extreme, standpoint. It is not as though we see the reliable middle-ground solution attacked by a massive capitalised lobby intended to convert us to a diet of chemical food, no matter what happens to our health. The 'opponent' is not the rational consensus at all; it is instead an equally forceful, comparably extreme view that seeks to propagandise the idea that the establishment is out to get us, and that only massive civil action can recapture the advantage for the hapless domestic consumer.

The problem is compounded by the reliance on the findings of traditional science. But I am of the view that science is leading us astray. Science is concerned with the repeatable realities of the type of phenomena you may test at the laboratory bench, and human meals do not come into this category.

The problem lies in the nature of cause and effect. If you put a light to a critical mixture of aluminium and iron oxide then it will burn at a temperature that is high enough to melt steel. That is science. But in the field of food there are no such simple answers. Here we might find a tribe that never suffers from bowel cancer, and eats nothing but raw vegetables. 'The answer is obvious,' says the campaigner. 'The ignition of the critical mixture caused the reaction in the first example, and the vegetarian diet caused the lack of cancer in the second case.'

That is where the difficulties start. The first part of that response is perfectly correct, and that is what science is all about. But the second is much more complex than it appears. It could be that those tribespeople obtain a specific anti-cancer compound in their dietary intake; it could be that vegetables protect against cancer; it might be that they are genetically resistant to the disease; it is possible they are better at controlling cancers because of some unknown auto-immune mechanism; perhaps they have a witch-doctor who charms away the disease; possibly they have a religious belief that confers resistance to cancers as a whole; the rocks on which they live may give out an anti-cancer vapour that protects them all; they may have been visited by spacemen in previous centuries and granted a life free from malignancies . . . and so on.

It is safe to suggest that most people would not give too much credence to the 'visitors from space' theory, but that's not the point. What matters is that:

a)   the various possibilities have differing degrees of likely validity;

b)   we do not have any way of telling which one is the 'truth';

c)   in the current trend of informed opinion, most people would accept the 'vegetarian diet' implication as the likely answer, without considering that there might be alternatives;

d)   in fact the 'vegetarian diet' hypothesis is not the most likely of the list, on present evidence;

e)   the 'single answer' may not exist at all;

f)   and, even if it does, it may be something to which we have not even referred. There could easily be some unrecognised aspect

8

of the tribespeople's life-style which causes the phenomenon of cancer-resistance.

In fact, the 'vegetarian diet' theory seems to me an unlikely answer. Vegetarians are not by any means 'immune' from cancer – whilst tribespeople in primitive societies are often less likely to suffer from cancers even if they eat a mixed, omnivorous diet. So the chances are that it is something else in the pattern of life that would be responsible.

The difficulty is that we place altogether too much faith in a false view of 'science' to provide answers. There is evidence to suggest that sugar is a useful substance, yet plenty of individuals who argue it causes a range of conditions from malignant hyperactivity and antisocial behaviour to tumours. There is a school of thought which argues that cholesterol in the diet causes arterial disease and death through heart attacks; but the equally convinced opposition retorts that cholesterol is produced by the body and is anyway vital for life. People claim that salt raises the blood pressure if eaten to excess; but there is evidence, too, that a *lack* of salt in the diet produces similar effects. We are sometimes enjoined to eat protein as a means of keeping healthy, whilst other campaigners insist that protein causes many of the world's ills. Some people insist that all additives should be banned, but food would be unhealthily dangerous if they all went. And we can think back to the days when people who insisted on eating bran cereals for breakfast were nothing more than cranks with a rectal-fixation, and contrast that with the current weight of evidence that goes so far as to suggest that roughage can even protect against heart attacks.

Science has not kept up with the demands of modern people for real facts and honest opinions. We wait for 'scientific evidence of harm' before we consider cutting back on violent movies, for instance, whilst we are willing to undertake wholesale changes in our daily lives based on the flimsiest of opinions. All the while we have a sixteenth-century narrow-mindedness about the unacceptable opinion. We are quick to complain about university meetings barracked by student activists who wish to silence the views – freely expressed and very likely honestly held – of extremists of one side, whilst allowing the opposition free rein. But how often do we stop to consider the unfashionable views, no matter how sound they may be? We look with horror at a Warsaw Pact decision to silence some spokesman of an unacceptable political movement in a nation that simply cannot bear criticism, but in our own daily decision-making we act just as narrow-mindedly. As this book was being compiled, a television programme was put together which argued against fat as a principle cause of heart attacks in human beings. It was said that there were some errors in the programme, and that some parts of it might be misconstrued – views that apply to many programmes, and to most on medical topics. Now, it *is* true that there is no direct evidence which links fat intake with heart disease, for the data that are available are both circumstantial and not overwhelmingly convincing (a point to which we return). It is also true that the conventional wisdom – that fat is thoroughly bad for you, is the fashionable view of the age.

So, was the programme seen in that light, as an answer to one extreme view through the posing of another? No, it was not. Instead, the programme was taken out of the schedules. This was a form of censorship that we rarely see in the field of extremist politics, but which is perfectly acceptable, it seems, if a fashionable dogma is to be challenged. It is not as though the view is an extreme one, for it is not; it is a view held by a very significant proportion of medical opinion. It is not as though it was an insubstantial opinion, for the evidence is at least as good on this side as it is on the other.

No: all that happened was that the view did not match the trendy orthodoxies of the establishment, and so it was cancelled. No longer need we look back to Galileo's time for examples of the need to toe the fashionable line. We are doing it ourselves in the 1980s, and with just as much fervour and unthinking conformity as any religious zealot of centuries ago. Science has no ability to tackle such complexities – and we have still a high level of prejudice and bias against new and unfashionable views. That is why I feel we need to move on to a state where we can put science, and what we call 'scientific evidence', into perspective; and where we can start a new openness of enquiry and an honesty of purpose which today's intensely polarised and fashion-conscious establishment seems so far to reject. It is reasonable to condemn the high-pressure lobby of the food industry when it seeks to off-load the products of a subsidised farming business onto people who may not want the products, might not benefit from them, and might even be harmed by them. But it is equally fair to criticise the unreasonable quasi-political theorising that is used by the opponents of industry in setting up campaigns of fear and societal unease for reasons that are similarly extreme.

Many of the traditional views on which our opinions are based do not hold water. One is that people eat what their parents ate, and have their tastes permanently instilled at the parental knee. This is far from the observable truth. In a matter of years we have seen ethnic restaurants gain ground in Britain, and exotic ingredients take root in the USA. Londoners who ate tripe and onions followed by bread and butter pudding must be astonished at the popularity of Chinese and Indian food – not as a luxury, but as a mainstay of everyday life. Pizzas appear in school menus where they were not even heard of in Britain a few decades ago. Lasagne, a stranger to British ears in the 1960s, is an everyday item of diet today. People at fruit stalls now buy kumquats and mangosteens, lychees and Chinese gooseberries (renamed 'kiwi fruit') with the durian, plaintains and sharon fruit (as the persimmon is now known). The dining table in the US is decorated, like never before, with shii-take fungi, scarlet radicchio and dried tomatoes, arugula and Piedmontese truffles.

Of course people are influenced by current trends, and we should always have known that: how did the turkey become so popular, and why else did hot curry come to feature in the British menu when people eat out?

We are all convinced that fat people are greedy and unhealthy (when I say 'all', I exclude many fat people – though a large number of those among us who are obese *do* feel that they are somehow inferior, sick people because of it). As I shall explain more fully later, fat people are often consuming no more than the rest of us. Most of them are certainly not fat because they are greedy, but because they function differently. Neither are they inevitably unhealthy. Take two people with an uncomplicated background – I mean by this that they are both free of diabetes, that neither has a genetic predisposition to excess cholesterol in the blood – but one of whom is fat, whilst the other is thin. The statistics suggest that both stand a similar chance of suffering a heart attack.

People accept that we are, in developed communities, generally overweight. Not so. The statistics may scream that one-third of us are overweight because we all eat too much, but to me there is a very different conclusion that might be drawn, and which is more intriguing by far. It is this: clearly (if the figures are right) even

11

though we all tend to eat too much, *two-thirds of us are not overweight*. The same data provide this seemingly unacceptable conclusion. To me, that is much more interesting.

We imagine that a fresh, crisp salad with farmhouse cheese is far more healthy than fried fish and chips. About the exact nature of 'healthiness' we might argue, but might you mean – in this context – 'less fattening'? Wrong: the cheese and salad is probably much higher in calories than the fish and french fries. 'Lower in unhealthy fats' then? Wrong again, I fear; cheeses as a rule are rich in saturated animal fats, whilst if your plaice was fried in polyunsaturated cooking oil then it would give you a double dose of 'health' (fish may contain components that act against the scourge of a heart attack). And if the fish meal was served with those hi-tech monsters frozen peas, whilst the salad contained an unhealthy specimen of celery, then it wins on another score too – stressed celery is a potent source of carcinogens (i.e. chemical substances that can initiate the transformation of a normal living cell to one that is malignant).

The health-giving cheese salad may be a highly fattening dish, rich in saturated animal fats and laced with cancer-causing agents, when compared with the fried fish and potato alternative. Yet on which one would you have placed your choice?

Cancer is an interesting example of the way fashions change. Decades ago and it was the threat of cancer that lay behind the campaign against manufactured foods. In many of the recent reports on healthy eating, cancer is not even mentioned. Now the emphasis is on heart attacks and blood pressure. Oddly enough, the current trend towards vegetables like beans is leading us towards one of the most well-documented sources of carcinogenic compounds. There are toxic substances in many vegetables, and potent mutagens (i.e. mutation-causing compounds) are formed in beans when fungi contaminate them. One class of these, the afla-toxins, is often found in beans and peanut products and is poten-tially very dangerous.

And there is a marked trend in controversies over nutrition – the manner in which polarisation leads to consequences that can be even more hazardous than what we were trying to avoid. It would be tragic if poeple, driven to eat a class of food in some temporary outbreak of campaigning zeal, suffered in consequence. Yet such swings do occur, and for the worst of reasons; the banning of cyclamates as artificial sweeteners in the United States is an example. It was claimed that cyclamates caused cancer in rats, and the Food and Drugs Administration have to ban from use any new product against which this is proved.

Many of the details of the experiments were later challenged, until the point when I think it would be fair to say that the case against cyclamates was not very sound. Alongside such dietary constituents as cress, celery, kippers, hamburgers and cups of tea, then cyclamates rate quite favourably in the cancer-causing stakes and seem far less threatening than many of the traditional foods we eat without compunction. Be that as maybe, the effect of the ban on cyclamates was to lead to a considerable increase in the amount of sugar as used as a sweetener instead. Yet – so perverse is the way these controversies work – there was a far more widely accepted case at the time against sugar! I am not saying that the anti-sugar arguments were sound, nor that they ought to be accepted; all I am saying is that *at the time* the establishment seemed to consider sugar a bigger threat to human health than cyclamates. So the ban was driving people to use an alternative that was widely held to be considerably worse.

Why are we so irrational, and how is it we can tolerate such strange twists in opinion and this continuing polarisation of views? People have always needed codes of identifiable criteria by which to select their notions of reality, and those who do not accept the norm are readily identified as unwanted and seem to attract a profound level of dislike. The norm changes from time to time, of course; and we can see many parallels with the food business in other walks of life. For instance, how would you accept the following statement? 'Blacks are everywhere. I cannot make up my mind whether they are a curse put there to annoy us, a joke by God against our kind, or a necessary evil.' That view might have seemed perfectly acceptable in British or American society a decade or two ago. It might be just as acceptable today in white sections of South Africa, and it is still a viewpoint to which some Australians adhere. In other words, this sentiment – which seems totally unacceptable to us in the current views of our era – was once much less offensive to whites, and is still inoffensive to whites in other places. Views do not have an absolute validity, then, but a shift in a little time, or across to a different culture, can make the inadmissable become acceptable again.

I quoted those sentiments for a good reason – they were not merely made up for this section of my discussion, put there to

13

shock. In fact they were recently said on a public platform. But the speaker was a woman, and the word 'blacks' was actually 'men'. In this way we can see how violent are the extremes of our polarised society, for such sentiments would have seemed entirely unacceptable a few years ago, and if they were expressed about a different target – like blacks, asians, catholics or jews – they would probably be unlawful today. The point is that in a few years they will seem equally anachronistic. That is what you must bear in mind.

The exacerbation of extreme opinions about food follows similar swings. That is why – though it is perfectly all right to say that fat is bad for you, and should be curtailed before it gives you a heart attack – you simply cannot say that fat is largely innocuous, and probably does no harm to the average adult. It is not that the facts are less provable, or that the evidence is too tenuous, for those objections would apply just as much to the alternative trendy veiwpoint. Though science has not realised it yet, facts matter very much less than do the interpretations we arbitrarily place upon them. When we add to that the virtual inability of science to demonstrate what might be construed as a 'fact' in nutritional research, then surely we can see that the waving of placards in this unceasing war of empty words is probably due for a change.

It is time that reason, sense and judgement entered the race, for the strictures of science have had their day. There is no scientific meaning to dietary requirements, for instance. We do not know what people require in their diets, even if we can often demonstrate the side-effects of an abnormal intake of food. Science cannot say what are the nutrient needs of individual people. Indeed we cannot even lay down what is necessary in a basic diet. Vitamins are an example – vitamin A is unnecessary if you consume *beta*-carotene from which it can be made in the body; vitamin D is synthesised in the skin by the action of sunlight; nicotinic acid (the B vitamin) can be substituted by tryptophan; vitamin C can be substituted by iso-ascorbic acid; and even the essential fatty acids could probably be replaced by the corresponding keto acids too . . . and so on. Even water, that common denominator of all life, can be made in the body by the oxidation of fat and carbohydrate. Little wonder those babies, pulled after a week and more from the remains of earthquake-shattered hospitals during 1985, managed to switch their metabolic processes to the pathways that remained, surviving in conditions that medical science might have said was impossible.

14

Babies have a need for such survival. In primitive societies the weaning of a baby from the breast to solid food was not the simple matter it is for us; and the establishment of a baby in breast feeding cannot have been reliable under such conditions. No doubt the ability to survive was a reminder of how babies kept going during the first traumatic weeks of life in the open air before outside aid became available. They remind us what is really the correct diet for human beings: breast-milk. Nothing else we consume is as self-evidently good for us.

Even here, when human life is just beginning, can we see the dangerous swings in fashionable views that have wrought havoc on human health over the years. Not so long ago the trend was away from breast-feeding altogether. This was an undesirable move for many reasons. One of those is that babies can develop an intolerance of dairy products that leads to ill-health in adult life. In fact it is easier to erect a medical case against dairy produce than it is to condemn many of the current dietary targets, a matter to which I will return. Another is the composition of cow's milk, on which substitutes have been based. Cow's milk contains more than 300% as much sodium as human breast milk, which is close to the upper limit that a baby's kidneys can excrete. If a baby drinking cow's milk is losing water through perspiration or diarrhoea, for instance, then the level of sodium in the blood serum can become dangerously high.

The ratio of phosphorus to calcium is also unfavourable in cow's milk, so far as human babies are concerned. Phosphorus was absorbed so readily by babies fed on cow's milk that they could not excrete the surplus. The serum phosphorus rose too high, the levels of calcium fell correspondingly, and some babies developed tetanus caused by the low calcium levels in their bloodstream.

Only about three decades ago, the contemporaneous fashion was to cause babies to have levels of calcium that were too high! At that time the vogue was to dose them with vitamin D. The vitamin came at them from almost every direction – from fortified drink, from mushy fortified cereals, from cod liver oil supplements – and it was possible for an infant to ingest as much as 100μg of vitamin D a day. That is ten times the recommended daily requirement of 10μg. In susceptible infants the levels of blood calcium rose too high, they lost their appetite and failed to develop normally. Only intervention from paediatric specialists faced with sick children brought about a reduction in the high levels that were being administered.

Even here there is a kind of swing in the opposite direction, for a *lack* of vitamin D causes rickets and this medieval-sounding condition is still with us. It occurs in some 1–3% of the child population in Britain, for example, most particularly in the babies of immigrant asian families. The vitamin is synthesised in the skin through the action of sunlight, as mentioned above, and these children often go out into the sunlight less than their British counterparts. If you would like to see yet another twist in the continuing skein of argument, then I should add that giving vitamin D as a supplement does not necessarily solve the problem either. To become active in the body, the vitamin needs to be chemically changed into the 25-hydroxy derivative; this occurs in the liver, and is less likely to happen in the tiny infants who are most at risk. If the baby is premature then the inability to undertake this metabolic change is even more marked. So here is another elusive strand in the argument – rectifying a deficiency in the diet does not necessarily solve the problem.

To a newborn baby, there is something even more important than milk. That is colostrum, the translucent liquid secreted by the mother during the commencement of breast-feeding her baby. Colostrum is highly charged with antibodies which the baby may need to fight an infection. It has been said that nearly half the protein in colostrum is in the form of antibodies which act against both viruses and bacteria in the intestinal tract. Also present is the antibacterial lysozyme (studied by Alexander Fleming, and responsible for alerting his mind to the possibility of antibiosis, on which he was later to publish with such well-known effect). There is moreover a substance which helps bind iron during the early days of subsistence as a free-living baby. This is lactoferrin, and nothing like it occurs in baby foods. Even breast milk is seriously deficient in iron, compared with the levels of input that the foetus received from the mother's blood supply, and the effect of early ingestion of lactoferrin from colostrum can make all the difference in benefiting from what is consumed.

The principal conclusion we may have to draw is that, in spite of what we do to ourselves, in the end nature and the constraints of our devlopment through the ages have given us inbuilt mechanisms to look after ourselves that are more difficult to overcome than you might imagine. Early in 1985 a report from West Africa showed how wrong we were to assume that pregnant women need to consume a greatly increased amount of food to nourish themselves and their developing baby, for example. Here were populations of black women consuming far fewer extra calories during pregnancy than the evidence suggested they *should* have been eating. As much as 80,000 additional calories were believed to be necessary over the nine months, half to lay down fat stores which would later be utilised in the production of breast-milk, and half to sustain the additional metabolic load during pregnancy itself. The African communities had no such extra input, and so they were given an energy-rich supplement to bring them nearer the expectations of the European medical specialists.

The result? As you might by now anticipate, they did not respond as they were expected to. The women who were fed the supplement, who were the healthiest of the group, who produced babies of the weights you would expect of well-nourished European women; this core of the sample actually utilised a mere 8000 extra calories out of what was provided in their food. For them, this additional input was all they could contain – it was one-tenth of what was predicted.

One can confound predictions after the baby is born, too. It is widely accepted that overfeeding a baby leads to obesity in later life. Indeed one nutritionist spokesman has often said that you can make a person any shape you wish, as an adult, by modifying the diet that the individual has during childhood. I do not accept that for a moment, and recent evidence suggests that babies control their own weight far more efficiently from within than we can attempt to do from outside.

To begin with, the laying down of fat reserves is normal during the first six months or so of life after birth. It is not just that there is an absolute increase, for the proportions go up: a baby at birth is about 15% fat, compared with 25% at 4 months of age. But several recent investigations suggest that there is no direct correlation between the weight of a baby and its weight as an infant. Certainly, there are fat babies who are still fat when aged eight. This is widely accepted, but it has been understood to be the inevitable fate of fat babies. That, it seems, is not true. Many of the overweight babies had moved down to the normal level by the age of 7–8, without anyone from outside intervening with diets. Many of the fat infants at eight years of age were actually of low weight as infants aged just a few months. And a follow-up study of over 100 infants by the time they were teenagers failed to show any relationship between the amount of fat they stored as infants, and the amount of obesity they exhibited in their teens.

What has been shown is that fat mothers often have fat babies. Obesity can run in families. It may be genetic. So the way we develop as babies, the manner in which we grow into adults, and the mechanisms by which we become the weight and shape we do; all these may be less easily influenced by outside factors than we like to imagine. In my view there may even be a discernible *purpose* in obesity. Babies are susceptible to wasting diseases, as are the elderly. I would suggest that the reason we find extra levels of stored fat during these extremes of life is in some instances a prophylaxis against the burdens of disease. An old person, like a two-month-old baby, may suffer a wasting disease and feel disinclined to eat just when this is vitally important. To a little child, fighting off the debilitating effect of some intestinal disorder, for instance, a store of extra energy reserves might be a life-saver. To an older and inactive person, reserves of fat can act as an internal food buffer to ward off the effects of disease whilst the body tries to work its way back to health.

And as for the fat people who eat no more than their fellows? Of course they are not 'greedy'. They are built that way, just as some are tall and some are short. You can stretch the legs to make short people longer, if you wish; you could doubtless stunt the growth of tall people to keep us all at average height. But the tuning of the bodily metabolism is an internal matter and, though you can inevitably limit weight gain by a restriction in dietary intake, we have to put into the balance the stress burden of worrying about what we eat. Though you may argue the merits of the case against sugar, the case for fat, the evidence in favour of those natural foods or the data against using vitamin supplements, nobody can pretend that stress is harmless. The stress of frustration and the inability to control an individual destiny may be killing more people than the dietary and environmental hazards put together.

This is one of my main targets: to help provide enough of an understanding for a reader to stop worrying about his or her diet. It is a paradox with which we have yet to tangle – but though we might argue about the risks attached to lipids (fats) or sugar in food, we would have to agree that stress, worry and frustration are bad for you. Listing the hidden dangers that might get you when your back is turned, and campaigning for the recognition of some untried hypothetical hazard lurking in your food, can itself add to ill-health. No matter how fervently you believe that someone who is overweight is heading for illness, once you add to that person's inner store of guilt by lambasting them with the latest threats, you are replacing the possibility that they are harming themselves with the certainty that *you* are harming *them*. I am certain that it is the modern style of life, to which so many people cannot adapt, which causes the bulk of our problems. If we could conquer that, we would be half-way to a healthier life for everyone.

If we look *behind* our beliefs for a change, we can start to understand the basis for them. In some ways we have grown up with an erroneous sense of right and wrong. For instance there is an unreasoned dislike of 'refined' foods. I say 'unreasoned' deliberately – it is not as though it takes scientific insight to know the difference, rather that some people seem to have a psychological distrust of foods that are white and pure. Take sugar as an example. As you will know if ever you use a sprinkling of sugar to revive a flagging fire, it is a potent source of energy. An ounce of sugar (30g) represents 110 calories (420 kilojoules). Liberated within your body through the metabolic conversion process that takes place within your cells, this is a concentrated form of energy for life.

At once we can perceive the way in which our values are subject to the whims of fashion. A decade and more ago we imagined that sugar was a valuable boost to our reserves. Products like Mars bars were sold because of their capacity to give extra energy, based on their sugar content. You are very likely nodding in agreement at this very moment – my, how ideas change! At this time amongst the best-selling commercial products are the breakfast cereals, all specifically designed ('tuned up', I even heard someone say) to meet the needs of busy executives who jog in the lunch hour. These are predominantly carbohydrate, and added sugar is one of the prime ingredients. So do not be too hasty when you condemn a seemingly unfashionable belief. Whilst it may be that you, as an individual, are aware of the hidden face of these expensively marketed products, tens of millions of people are not so thoughtful. Such cereals, with their added sugar and colourants, are selling like never before. Even if Mars bars have changed the wording, emphasising the help with 'work, rest and play' that every such food obviously confers on the consumer, there are manufacturers who continue to equate carbohydrates with energy, and who sell them on that basis to the very people who claim to be most aware of the need for health. A Mars bar, for example, and 100g of Weetabix contain similar levels of calories.

The evidence over the safety of sugar is a matter we could debate for more pages than there are in this book. I do not believe that there is any sound case to make out for a belief that sugar causes cancer, though it certainly encourages the development of dental caries. There have been newspaper reports in recent years that sugar causes abnormal or antisocial behaviour, though there is very little evidence to support that view. The newspaper features I have read on this topic all stem from data which appeared in the *International Journal of Biosocial Research* during the 1980s and with such a pedigree you might be inclined to accept them (the journalists were so inclined, after all). Yet it seems that this journal is impossible to find in the British academic libraries. Vincent Marks, Professor of Clinical Biochemistry at the University of Surrey, found a copy in the United States but he has never seen it in Britain. The journal claims to be abstracted in *Psychology Abstracts*, but there is no such publication. There is a journal with the title *Psychological Abstracts* but Dr Marks says that it does not cover the *International Journal of Biosocial Research*. And the findings on sugar in this elusive little publication? They relate to personality and behaviour changes in groups of prisoners given a change of diet. The 'junk food' and the added sugar were cut.

Obviously there are problems here, partly because of the small sample, added to the difficulty of assessing what you mean by good and bad behaviour. There is also what I call *parallel causality*, of which we will see more examples in this book. This is the mechanism by which behavioural criteria can be altered by attitudinal changes consequent upon a new regime. It works, I suggest, like this: a new diet or a new approach is introduced, and any results are seen as the consequence of that change. But there is a second line of reaction that could be the cause – namely, the altered consciousness that led to the introduction of the change. It might not be that, if you buy pills and stick to their use, *they* are responsible for your improved health, trimmer waistline, boosted confidence, for there is a further factor to take into account. Namely, your altered attitude. It could be that the very act of buying pills and taking them indicates a new sense of resolve or of purposefulness which you have previously lacked. In my view we should start to consider that aspect.

It could certainly apply to persons given a new dietary regimen. The very fact that something is being tried to improve conditions could itself trigger a lessening of tensions, and does *not* have to be consequent upon the psychopharmacological manifestations of the new diet. So here we have a case where we have:

- data from a small sample
- subjectively-assessed behavioural results
- published in an obscure journal
- ignoring an equally plausible alternative mechanism of causality . . .

yet that did nothing to stop the newspapers from publicising the view that sugar was a leading cause of anti-social behaviour. Compare that with the arguments against fat and heart attacks (which led to a TV programme being summarily cancelled) and we can see how the public consciousness is prey to the fashionable views held at any one time by the establishment. 'Facts' and 'figures' on that basis stand nowhere, alongside the subjective force of what elsewhere I have called *fashionism*.

As a matter of personal judgement I do not think that added sugar is a sensible item to consume in our daily diets. It often masks delicate flavours, it encourages tooth decay, it provides additional calories which most people these days like to control; and that before we consider the various medical questions about excessive sugar in the diet. However, this is not what the antagonists of sugar are campaigning about. The health-food fads are not so much against sugar, but against *refined* sugar. It is a revulsion against white, pure sucrose. Instead the adherents to this view sweeten their drinks with honey or use brown sugar, described as *unrefined*. But honey and brown sugar are both giving you sugar, the same sucrose. I cannot see how you can have it both ways. Either sugar is acceptable, or it isn't. Eating the same material in a slightly different coloured presentation is valueless, if you are a member of the anti-sugar movement.

Calling brown sugar 'unrefined' is fundamentally incorrect. All crystalline sugar is refined. White sugar has undergone a final purification process whilst brown sugar is still tainted with some of the byproducts of refinement. I could probably make out a stronger case against the consumption of those impurities than against the eating or drinking of sugar in the purified, white form. But no, it is the purity and the whiteness themselves which is the target of the revulsion, so much as the sugar.

It is much the same with bread. Here the target is white bread, the mass-produced sliced bread of the supermarket. More and more people instead buy brown bread. But brown bread is virtually the same, it is simply bread made from the same purified flour to which is added a little caramel as a colourant. Wholemeal bread is different again (and we will return to that in Chapter 7), and there is a clear case to be made out for eating the entire grain, rather than just a purified portion of it. The fact that bread causes much human suffering and is a widespread source of morbidity need not concern us here – nor need we become unduly euphoric about the supposed 'naturalness' of wholemeal bread. No bread is 'natural', which is perhaps why it makes so many people ill.

The essential point here, though, is that it is the *whiteness* against which people campaign. Yet where did the demand for white sugar and white bread originate? It is often seen as though the blame lay in the lap of an avaracious food manufacturing industry, forcing its wares on a hapless public. That is not so. In earlier centuries, sugar and flour were heavily contaminated with rodent droppings, bits of beetles, moths and bugs, dirt, dust and detritus – and all this before unscrupulous dealers sometimes added sawdust, borax or chalk to boost the volume of a profitable item of commerce. In those days, a pure product was the hallmark of safety, and white sugar, like white flour, gave some indication that many of the dangerous or simply unsavoury inclusions were absent. The demand for the white product was led by consumers anxious for purity.

It is just this purity, this whiteness, against which modern campaigners are exerting their arguments. They are not so much opposed to flour or to sugar, but to the *refinement*, so called. To my mind it may be acceptable to protest the virtues of a given way of life, or to propagandise against an item in the diet if you believe it to harm the consumer. But in these campaigns we have people eating brown sugar and brown bread for no good reason at all. It is almost enough to make one postulate that the turning away from *whiteness* could be explained by psychiatric theory. It has nothing to do with the nature of food, or its safety.

There is an historic origin for the bouncing (fat) baby against which we now so mightily protest. Infants in primitive societies suffer greatly from intestinal diseases which cause diarrhoea and wasting. Systemic conditions, like tuberculosis, have a similar propensity to waste the body tissues, producing a sad, listless and sunken-eyed child with a reduced likelihood of survival. Many of the pitiful faces of little children we have seen on TV programmes from starving drought stricken areas of the world are not showing the signs of mere 'starvation' at all, but are actually ill with one of these infections. The face of the child portrays vividly the misery of illness in one so young.

Bearing this in mind, you can easily imagine how in earlier times our forbears came to watch for signs of wasting as the harbinger of morbidity in little children. In those societies, an infant who was bouncing with chubby health had a clear advantage over one who was thin. So the association of 'fit' with 'fat' has clear and perfectly rational origins. And (if it is correct to argue that reserves of fat can sometimes be a helpful adjunct against disease, as I have suggested earlier) it is dangerous to try to argue that these traditional notions are muddleheaded and irresponsible.

Similarly biased attitudes extend right through to the language and approach of the official reports on food that appear from time to time. The NACNE report, for example, was heavy on criticism of foods as the culprit behind heart attacks, high blood pressure and other contentious issues whilst skating around the problems of cancer and cell mutation for which there is a growing body of evidence that could incriminate food. The 1984 COMA report included a short summary of recommendations to the industry, couched in deferential terms in a body of text that alluded to the need to 'consider', to 'enquire' and to 'consult', contrasting with a larger list of recommendations for the public, written in a commanding and imperious style with the key words set in eye-catching bold type. They virtually ignored out-of-home eating, which is not only an important source of food but – with restaurants and fast-food marketing on an upward trend – is becoming increasingly important.

There are traps for the unwary in official reports. Early in 1985 the London *Observer* published a summary critique of the modern diet and illustrated the point with a scientific-looking 'wheel of health' purporting to show how what we ate matched what we ought to be eating. At a glance it is the worst and most inaccurate 'graph' of the year. It equates essential fats with polyunsaturates,

23

which is not valid. It speaks of 'fibres', which is more like illiteracy. 'Fibres' are a microscopical feature of certain plant and animal tissues. What is measured in food intake is dietary *fibre*, a substance. The extra 's' alters the whole meaning completely (just as there is a world of difference between someone getting air, and somebody else giving themselves *airs*). It lists elements that include Ch and CL, neither of which exists*. And, although it purports to show how much we averagely eat, it neglects two important aspects of this fundamental question:

a)   It does not show overconsumption. There is a clear excess of fat in our diets over what we reasonably need, no matter how you look at it. Yet saturated fat does not show on the 'wheel' at all, and the filling of the segment for 'energy' suggests we are getting just what we need, whilst in fact we are eating more than that.

b)   The graph pretends to show how much we really need.

Yet we have no knowledge of what our requirements really are. You can give minimum daily requirements for some constitutents, but evidence is unrealiable. Levels of vitamin C that will cure scurvy are higher than those that will prevent it. Iron in the diet can sometimes be unavailable to the body. (Indeed one of the most widespread forms of iron given to pregnant women for many years has since been shown to be ignored by the body and excreted in the faeces.) Some vitamins are elaborated by microbes that live in the intestinal tract, and not only taken in with the diet. And past experience shows that official figures can often change with time, like the recommendations of dangerously high levels of vitamin D referred to on p 15. Putting these random ideas down as a loftily-named 'wheel of life' gives them a spurious authority, makes them look forbiddingly 'scientific'. They are not. They are inaccurate and do little but add to the burden of stress which is already killing us by the thousand.

---

*The 'Ch' appears to be *Cr*, chromium, whilst the 'CL' is probably *Cl*, chlorine. Though they may seem trivial differences to the non-scientist, they are actually a sign of gross ignorance, just as if an international political columnist writing about the Prime Minister of the UK wrote of: *Mr thatches, Prime Minister of the UB*.

CHAPTER TWO

One positive precept you might adopt in working out what to eat is to fit the diet to our evolutionary past. If we have developed with a given amount of roughage and a fixed proportion of protein, then keeping within those limits would make obvious sense. The stories of children eating nothing but biscuits and who drink nothing but tea are examples of what happens when the principle is neglected. The difficulty of this viewpoint, which I have used for years as a way of encouraging a rethink of our dietary priorities, is that so little of our diet is 'natural' for us. That is not only true of modern mankind, for it has been the case for many thousands (perhaps tens of thousands) of years.

A couple of centuries ago we were eating a good deal of bread and drinking beer. In the northern countries grains like oatmeal were popular and the potato increased in popularity more rapidly in the north of England, for example, than in the south. During the late 1700s tea was beginning to emerge as a popular drink but the typical pattern was for two meals a day to be primarily bread and beer in northern Europe, bread and wine in the southerly European latitudes. One meal a day was cooked, and in Britain this was the mid-day dinner.

We often look back at accounts of meals from centuries ago in Britain and marvel at how much they ate – bread and puddings, suet and starch – which would seem difficult to consume these days. One reason why they did eat a lot of highly calorific food may have been the need to fuel a warm body that was continually losing heat to the environment. We are more cosseted these days, and might have difficulty metabolising the excesses of a previous era. During the growth of the industrial age diets were less lavish. Data collected late in the 1700s suggest that people ate around 2000 calories and 50–60 grams of protein a day, which is rather less than they may have needed, on average.

We might hope to learn useful lessons if we go back in time, but mankind has been active as a genetic engineer and biotechnologist for millenia and it is hard to find much that *is* natural. Our domesticated animals are all species created by human intervention and have a higher satured fat content than wild creatures. Cereal crops have been created by genetic intervention too. They are species made by humans for their own expediency and are nothing like their long-lost ancestors. Even the popular fruits are the result of human intervention. Bananas and oranges have been created by our distant forbears, and the line through which they were developed has long since been lost.

Bread is made from the flour produced by milling grain, and milling itself is a profoundly unnatural process. The windmills from an earlier era that delight us in protected landscapes are technological wonders, working with the aid of wind power, and the action they undertake is an example of human intervention – processing an artificially created crop into a sophisticated item of diet. Flour, though, is unpalatable. To make it into bread it is fermented with the yeast microbe. As the yeast cells grow, the carbon dioxide (CO_2) they produce blows bubbles in the dough and creates a leavened loaf which is much tastier. The yeast fungus naturally grows on the skin of fruit, where it obtains sufficient sugar to sustain its life processes. No yeast ever comes into contact with flour in nature, for flour does not exist apart from where mankind has produced it. The harvesting of the energies of the yeast cell to make a glutinous dough into a foamy loaf of bread is biotechnology – and we have utilised it for thousands of years.

Biotechnology has given us brewing: wine and beer, those traditional mainstay drinks, result from ancient scientific expertise. We harness microbes to give us cheeses too, and the fermented milks from kumiss to yoghourt. The extraction of butter-fat by churning milk is technology, for butter (no matter how widespread its popularity throughout the world) is an entirely unnatural substance.

Our diet of meat, vegetables, fruit, bread and butter, cheese,

wine and beer is all composed of unnatural materials and technological products. There is, simply, nothing *of nature* (and hence
'natural') in it. Neither is there any basis in the idea that natural
foods are inherently good, no matter how you define the terms.
One of the most widespread staple foods in the world is cassava
and this root crop poisons the consumer with cyanide – unless the
food is cooked first, which boils away the offending constituents.
In fact, cassava is always cooked before being eaten, so it rarely
causes any problems for the consumer. But it is a vast annual
crop, is very 'natural', and kills you in the 'natural state'. Broad
beans can produce a condition in which a severe haemolytic
anaemia strikes down otherwise healthy consumers of broad beans.
The condition, known as *favism*, is found in the Mediterranean and
seems to be caused by a genetic inability on the part of some
people to produce enough of the enzyme glucose-6-phosphate
dehydrogenase – necessary for the broad beans to be properly
metabolised. Chick peas are associated with a form of spastic
paralysis of the legs. This condition is named *neurolathyrism* and is
named after the chick pea itself, *Lathyrus sativa*. Cycasin is a toxic
compound (a glycoside) produced by the nuts, leaves and roots of
the cycad plant from which flour is made throughout the tropics.
The populations which use it extensively know about the toxicity
and have evolved methods to eliminate the glucoside: they crush
and wash the nut before they grind it into flour, and this washes
away the toxin.

Experimental feeding of this toxin to animals has shown that
they are likely to develop tumours – and even that if pregnant rats
arc fed a diet containing such materials their offspring will develop
cancers later in life. There is a comparable component in oil of
sassafras, known as safrole, which is strongly carcinogenic in rats
and dogs. Over 90% of oil of sassafras is made up of this seemingly
dangerous component, which also occurs in nutmeg, mace and
cinnamon. But does this pose a problem for humans? Probably not:
there are no figures to suggest that safrole poses a real problem, and
a study of the Okinawa Islanders has shown that – although they
ate a lot of cycad products – they had no more liver cancer than
a control population who did not eat any. There are, in fact,
innumerable substances in our diet which seem to be a possible
hazard from one standpoint even if, from another, they have the
look of innocuousness about them. The simple idea that foods in
the natural state are inherently wholesome, whilst foods that have

27

been processed are instrinsically dangerous, has nothing to substantiate it.

There is, for example, a view that – since cooking does not exist in nature – raw foods are all you should eat. There is no merit in the idea. The digestion of cooked foods is generally easier than that of raw components, so cooking conveys an immediate benefit to the consumer of food. Cooking helps to sterilise food which may be contaminated by the organisms which can cause food-poisoning. Thirdly, cooking causes the hydrolysis and oxidation of some of the potentially dangerous molecules that might otherwise harm us (like the removal of the cyanide component from cassava). If a campaign to eat more raw food encouraged people to step up their daily intake of fruit and vegetables, then it would be in that sense a useful move. But 'rawness' is not itself useful, and it can cause an increased risk of disease.

What of vegetarianism? This principle has greatly increased in popularity over recent years and there is a school of thought which argues that meat eating is now on the way out – within a few score years, they claim, we will all be vegetarian. Let us first look at some of the claims. The view that seems to have gained credence is not merely that meat-eating is unhumanitarian or exploitive, it goes further than that. To the vegetarian, the idea is that this is the true state for humans, an intrinsically better way to live and more natural than the omnivorous state. But is vegetarianism a 'more natural' way to live? Let us examine the facts of the matter, which can enable us to elaborate a rational set of criteria.

Dentition

There are two main groups of mammals, the carnivores and the herbivores, eating meat and vegetation respectively. The dentition in the two is specialised to take account of the diet. The grinding of the teeth in herbivores has given them flat, broad teeth which grow quickly to replace what is worn away and which have in consequence a wide pulp canal well furnished with blood vessels, to nourish the continually growing teeth. Between the incisors which 'chop' the vegetation and the molars which grind it there is a marked gap. Such is the configuration of a typical herbivorous species – sheep, goats and cattle are examples.

In carnivores there is a quite different pattern. Here there is virtually no pulp cavity, the root of the tooth being closed. In the space between the incisors and the molars of carnivorous animals lies a sharp tooth for tearing meat, the carnassial. The premolars are somewhat sharpened and the crowns of the teeth are ridged and pointed.

Where does the human fit into this pattern? In our own case we find a half-way house.

The root canal at the apex of the tooth is small, but still open (which is why we get toothache). It is a compromise between the wide and open root canal of the herbivore and the absent canal typical of carnivorous animals. The crowns of the teeth are some-what fissured and sculpted, though not as much as in a carnivore. There is no gap between the incisors and the molars, as in the herbivores, but neither is there a well-marked carnassial tooth. Instead there is a moderately developed premolar, adequate for the handling of meat though not the kind of fearsome tooth you would find in a dog. These observations lead on to suspect that mankind lies half-way between the two types of configurations – between herbivores and carnivores. According to the evidence of the dentition, then, we might be supposed to be *omnivores* – i.e., intended to eat both kinds of food.

External Anatomy

Much of the design of the human body which we can observe from the outside is concerned with our habit of walking about on our hind legs (not a practical idea in every way, judging by the plague of backache which afflicts us). But there are lessons to be learned from the way our eyes are aligned. As a rule, herbivores have eyes on the sides of the head, looking outwards to provide a wide field of view. This is because it is the role of the herbivore, in the ecological scheme of things, to consume vegetation and then in turn to be consumed by a carnivore. Herbivores serve the purpose of converting grass into meat, and so the eyes are situated in the best place to keep a watch for predators. Carnivores have eyes that are better suited for hunting, rather than the avoidance of being hunted: their eyes are on the front of the head, in pairs where they provide the best stereoscopic vision. The rule is, then, that the hunter has eyes that look forward, whilst the hunted have eyes that look sideways. Humankind has eyes with the bias in favour of the carnivorous pattern.

Internal Anatomy

The most clear-cut case we can cite here is the appendix. In herbivorous animals the appendix is one of the larger organs in the abdomen. In rabbits, for instance, it dominates the abdominal cavity and plays an important role in food digestion. Inside the appendix thrives a population of microbes which can digest the cellulose of the grass on which the animal feeds. Rabbits lack the enzymes that can break down cellulose and enable them to digest the cell contents of grass and other vegetation, but the microbes they harbour can undertake this for them. The rabbits then digest the microbes, and in this way they obtain the nourishment from the grass diet.

In carnivores there is no such structure as an appendix. It simply does not exist. This provides a clear distinction between the two groups of mammals. Humankind occupies an intermediate position. In humans the appendix does exist, but it is a diminutive structure no larger than a little finger. And (as is often the case with rudimentary structures) it is liable to become diseased. This fact is of medical importance, and incidentally gave rise to one of the less well-known cases of fraud in the years before the Second World War. An American surgeon launched a private campaign for prophylactic appendectomy – the removal of the appendix in healthy young patients, so that they might avoid the possibility of contracting appendicitis in later life. Such ideas remain with us to this day. A more recent example has been prophylactic mastectomy, in which young women have had their breasts surgically removed before breast cancer had a chance to appear. The argument was that, since the only purpose of the breasts was to feed babies, and since all babies of the new generation were bottle-fed in any event, they might as well get rid of their breasts whilst they were young enough to withstand the operation. I shall not dwell on the gaps in the argument – but it does put the prophylactic appendectomy into some perspective, and makes it seem tame by comparison. At least there was nothing mutilative about that.

The way the surgeon in question carried out his work, there was nothing even traumatic about it, for he evolved the expedient of making a slight incision in the skin and simply suturing it closed again. He knew that appendicitis was a rare condition in healthy young people and he amassed a useful income by the simple technique of leaving out the surgery altogether. The patients were pleased, since they had the neatest scar imaginable. And matters continued thus until local doctors began to record spasmodic cases of appendicitis in patients who were on the record as having no appendix remaining! Eventually, the cases were tied together and the fraud unmasked. I use the term 'unmasked' with some hesitation, since, as is so often the way with self-regulating hierarchies, nothing was done to compensate the victims or to censure the perpetrator of this confidence trick. But the doctor who benefited from the appendix and its degenerate role in human affairs reminds us of the intermediate structure it adopts: it lies between the absent appendix of the carnivore and the massive organ typical of herbivorous creatures, and suggests that, on this evidence too, mankind is omnivorous.

This does not imply that people should not be vegetarians if they want to. If you object to the iniquitous lengths to which intensive farming goes in order to maximise profit for the producers – and with minimum thought for either the animals or their consumers – then on such humanitarian grounds the spread of vegetarianism rather further through the current of human affairs can only spread gentleness and sensibility. Many people say they find meat distasteful – another good reason to go vegetarian. We do not eat a great amount of meat in our family, as it happens, and there is a tendency for people to move away from the massive hunks of roast meat that used to grace the table at weekends.

But if, on the other hand, you feel that you must become a vegetarian because it is the natural state for humans then I believe you are on unsupportable ground. Evidence from many sources suggests that we developed to be omnivores and that this is the best way to remain healthy and well-nourished. There is an important lesson in this: not that you ought to eat meat if you do not wish to, but that vegetarianism is not the 'natural' way for us to thrive and so the change to a vegetarian diet needs thought, advice and planning. Since a diet of vegetation does not fit our bodies, for the reasons outlined, then you have to take special care when embarking on a vegetarian way of life to ensure that the foods you eat make up for the items – abundant in meat – which are now absent from your daily intake of food. When the diet

31

becomes stricter, and of a vegan character – omitting even eggs, fish and dairy produce – then that care must be redoubled. There are families which foist onto young children a dangerously limited diet of processed fruit in bottles and a little yoghourt, heedless of the way their babies become listless and disaffected in response. The infant mind and body needs a highly nourishing input during this formative phase of life, and depriving children of their right to a healthy diet is hazardous, and selfish to say the least.

The error some people make is to imagine that vegetarianism means simply leaving the meat out of your diet. That is a misconstruction. The real principle should be to *replace* the meat with something else which the individual finds acceptable so that the daily intake of food remains nourishing and balanced. In this way the approach becomes positive: 'What shall I eat to be healthy?' rather than negative: 'What must I reject to avoid disease?'

As for the quest for a 'natural diet' – there is not much to be gained from this concept in the popular sense. The only natural food for a human being is mother's breast milk, and that is rather low in iron and vitamin D. Everything else is obtained from outside sources, initially being obtained by parents, and then broadening as adult choices begin to encroach on a developing mind. Social awareness, palatability, fashion and expediency all come into the equation. You could try a palaeolithic diet, trapping wild creatures and pulling them apart with your fingers, supplementing that intake with a few nuts and berries (trusting that they are not poisonous) and gathering roots along the way. You could up date that approach and try the primitive vegetables and early crops of the neolithic era, or the fruity spiced-meat concoctions of the Middle Ages, designed to disguise the taste of putrescence as much as to enhance the flavour in a positive sense. There is no end to the possibilities . . . but none of it is 'natural'.

Our best hope is to build up an overview of nutrition so that we can make sensible, personal choices. I do not seek to encourage that you study the subject in exhaustive and obsessive detail, more that you build up what I speak of as a 'total vision' approach in which the principles are understood. The rest follows. But it is all founded on the criteria that happen to be fashionable at the time. For instance at present there is a vogue for the control of cholesterol in our diets. This is because fatty deposits containing this substance are found lining the clogged blood-vessels of the victims of arteriosclerosis, and raised levels of cholesterol in the bloodstream are regarded as unhealthy. But you must bear in mind that cholesterol is an important structural component in human cells. For instance, the insulation of the nerve cells is due to the deposits within the neurone walls of fatty substances like this. Cholesterol is necessary for health. Furthermore, it is known that the body manufactures cholesterol, in some people in excessive quantities. In addition, it has been shown that the levels in the blood are not causally related to the amounts in the diet: the cruicial cause-and-effect mechanism has not been demonstrated and there is some doubt whether it exists. In the present state of our understanding, then, it might be sensible to cut out foods which supply an excessive amount of cholesterol. But there is little to be gained from frightening people into a state of neurosis which is much more life-threatening than the condition about which you are protesting. And, above all, do remember that (just as starchy foods were anathema a few decades ago, whilst they are now at the mainstay of a balanced diet) it is still possible that cholesterol   today's scapegoat – could become tomorrow's wonder drug. Such volte-face situations have often occurred in the past. It might yet be that the fad diet of tomorrow will involve stepping up your fat intake (there has already been one diet founded on the principle EAT FAT TO GROW SLIM!) and it could turn out that the no-vegetable way to health, or the banana-and-roast-beef fitness plan, will yet make my words look out of date by the mid-1990s. Or even by two weeks next Thursday.

CHAPTER THREE

The question that bothers so many people is not just what food they are going to eat, but what other things they are going to consume as hidden extras. The buzz-word of the moment is *additives*. The question of food additives is complicated by the fact that the term is surrounded by powerful connotations – all negative. It is much the same as the aura of distastefulness which surrounds the term *chemical*. Yet all food is chemical in nature, so is the metabolic processing it undergoes in the body, and so too is the person who does the eating. Sprinkle a little pepper on your peas, or add a dash of cognac to your coffee, and nobody would consider that those were distasteful acts. But imagine how such actions would seem if couched in the biased terms I have quoted above. Ask your guest: 'Some additives for your peas?' or 'a little chemical in your coffee?' and the question does not sound the same.

The connotations of the term additive become clearer when we consider what additives do. Essentially, a food additive performs two possible tasks:

- it makes food safer, more nutritious or palatable;
- it makes a healthy profit for the producer/user.

In an ideal world, a specific food additive would satisfy all ends of the market network. As it is, there is a tendency for additives to be overused and mistrusted, and that can prevent us from appreciating what they can do to improve our lot.

Let us begin with a consideration of what happens to food between its maturation as a harvest and its consumption in a meal. Food can be oxidised. That has to be the case, or it would not be food in the ordinary sense. In order to be chemically assimilated by the processes of living cells in the human body the food needs to be chemically active, and it is perfectly possible for this chemical change to begin before the food has been eaten by the consumer. Sometimes the food is said to be 'off', but what does that term actually *mean?* In the finer senses it might mean that the foodstuff has undergone some kind of chemical alteration, like oxidation, a change of acidity (pH), produced by the air or even by the action of sunlight, which can affect some foods adversely.

A food can 'go off' without any of these changes. During the filming of the television series *Food For Thought* we put together a display of all the eggs you eat in a year, and we had a great pile of eggs in cartons stacked up in a warehouse in Wiltshire. Unfortunately the building had been used for the storage of some odoriferous bags of fertiliser the week before, and the smell had lingered. It did not bother us too much, for it was the kind of odour that deadened the nostrils and was soon ignored by the crew, after the first phase of acclimatisation was over. At the end of the shoot the eggs had acquired the aroma of the warehouse. There was no harm done to them chemically – they were just as nourishing as they were to begin with – they had simply adsorbed the smell of the fertiliser and it clung to them tenaciously. Nothing could shake it off. By the time the suppliers came to collect the eggs they were essentially unusable for normal culinary purposes – an interesting example of how foods can 'go off' without any actual change in their nutritional composition.

Normally food that is 'off' has been subjected to bacterial decay. Microbes can metabolise foods just as we hope to do ourselves, for they are comparable living organisms with similar processes to our own. As the microbes proliferate they can alter the taste, appearance, and safety of the food. Often a change in aroma is the first sign that something has gone wrong. Food that has changed in this way may be distasteful; in some cases (when a cheese is being metabolised by a blue fungus, for instance) the change may bring about a marked improvement; sometimes the alteration can lead to food poisoning and the danger of disease.

For thousands of years our forebears have searched for ways to minimise these hazards. Jams are made with sugar at such a high concentration that fungi cannot proliferate, and so they are a useful way of storing away fruits in a palatable form. Salted meats prevent bacteria from reproducing and so help provide valuable protein supplies through the winter in societies without advanced methods of food storage. Dried fish removes the water that microbes need to survive, and allows the food to be kept palatable for prolonged periods . . . and food additives have often been used to prevent the oxidation of food in store.

You might feel that, if a food additive can act against food-spoiling organisms, surely it must act against people. That is not a fair comparison. Firstly, modern additives are specifically selected because of their ability to affect micro-organisms whilst leaving the human consumer largely alone. Food manufacturers are well aware of the dire consequences that lie in wait for anyone marketing a food that has undesirable effects on the consumer, and for that reason as much as for pure altruism they ensure that additives are relatively safe for people, just as they are relatively lethal for microbes.

The second reason why the assumption is not reasonable is that the addition of a preservative to a food means that the organism which wishes to metabolise the food finds its entire environment has been made unavailable for it. To a microbe, a slice of cured bacon is its entire planet, and none of it is available for use as a food. To you, as the human consumer, the bacon is only a small portion of your environment and the trace of preservative you may ingest is millions of times less threatening to you than it is to the bacterium that would otherwise have got there first. For this reason the antioxidants in food do not have the same effects on the consumer as they are intended to have on the microbes.

The development of antioxidants has been a profound step forward in the provision of safe food, and not only because they help preserve food against going 'off'. Fats can undergo oxidative changes which result in their becoming rancid. Rancid fats are a potent source of the kinds of chemicals associated with cancer and mutation in living cells. We do not need to fear them unduly (the body acts against cancer-causing chemicals, as we will see later in Chapter 7) but there are good reasons for avoiding rancidity if we can. Antioxidants in food are an important means of preventing them from forming undesirable, even dangerous, by-products of spoliation, and no matter how well the body deals with these chemicals it makes good sense to avoid them if we can.

36

Other additives provide extra levels of nutriment in foods that lack them, or they improve texture, making foods more palatable; so additives are not merely 'bad news'. You should not allow yourself to be unconditionally anti-additive, for without them we would have food that was dangerous to eat. The problem is that once an industry has become established it tends to attract its own momentum and becomes self-perpetuating until it mushrooms out of all proportion. This is what has happened to the food additive industry. Once additives have been proven to be a profitable side-line and then a sound commercial mainstream enterprise, the need to produce more and different additives becomes the priority. The need to sell them to more and more manufacturers follows closely behind.

There is nothing inherently evil in all this – I doubt whether you were working today out of pure love of the exercise – since in a materialistic age like ours people seem to like making money for themselves, whether it is by founding a megabuck industrial complex, or driving a taxi and spending weekends on the golf course. As I see it, the problems arise when you have a switch-over in criteria: when the desire to correct a problem and satisfy a need becomes instead a craving to expand an industry-led enterprise. Whereas you began with a system intended to make our food safer, you end up with something very different – a phase when the principal motive is to produce increasingly profitable additives, and to sell them to ever more manufacturers. We now enter an age where the expediency becomes centred on a race for financial solvency and commercial expansion, whilst the interests of the consumer disappear at the back.

My own belief is that additives are over-used by the food industry in consequence of this phase gathering its own momentum. There are over 3,000 additives in use, whilst perhaps 100 are truly necessary. If people refuse to eat processed vegetables, say, because the colour is repellent, then let us use some safe green colourant if it will help the customers benefit from a valuable food they would otherwise reject. But the issue becomes very different when manufacturers try to sell an ever-growing range of products. Then we have a system where people find green colour in every possible vegetable product, even if the traditional version was quite green enough to be acceptable. There are fruit products on the market which contain a mélange of artificial additives, designed to boost colour and taste; but alongside these you can find the same kind of product – with none of the additives – which is just as appetising and equally good for you, without the need for outside interference. When I see similar products alongside each other and have a chance to try them, then I even think that the 'unadulterated' version has more appeal and just a hint more fruitiness than the additive-containing alternative.

That, you may say, is just a subjective judgement. So it is. And I would add that the judgement is very likely clouded by one's knowledge of the fact that one of the products is the genuine article, whilst the other contains some superfluous additions. But that does not invalidate the point! If the knowledge that a product is additive-free can possibly make me appreciate it just a little more, then there would be a good case to be made for boosting sales of the product by leaving out the additives. I know that my children have been put off drinking Ribena since they noticed the artificial colour it contained, as they know perfectly well how strong is the colour of freshly pressed blackcurrant juice. If a product so intensely purple needs colour to make it saleable (even when it comes in a cardboard carton) then the instinctive reaction is to suspect the processing it has had to undergo. There are survey data that tend to suggest other people feel the same way – a Consumers' Association report in 1983 showed that 62% of respondents would decide not to buy a given product because of what they saw on the listed ingredients.

The scientific end of the additives field tends to be enthusiastic about their merits. Thus the Director of the Leatherhead Food Research Association has stated that: 'The public could be forgiven [for thinking] that the food industry is maximising the use of additives solely for its own ends with no regard for the fate of the ultimate consumers. All of us concerned with the food industry know this to be completely untrue.' (*Sunday Times Magazine*, 27 October 1985.) That is not my view. I am certain the industry *is* maximising its use of additives, and that the research scientists who depend on the investigations in this field for their livelihood are very positive about the need for that to continue. The key phrase is 'with no regard for the fate of the ultimate consumers'. Of course they are so concerned – the consumers would be quick to sue if they discovered they were damaged by a food product, and that is the most electrifying prospect for anyone charged with looking for unwanted side-effects. If the view were to be shortened to the possibility that the industry was 'maximising the use of

38

additives *largely* for its own ends' then it might not be so easy to insist that nobody thought it was true. A similar statement has come from the Consumers' Association: 'There is no evidence that food additives are a major risk to people generally.' As far as I am aware, that is true – but only because of the ingenious choice of words. The risk is not 'major', but it may yet prove to be 'significant'; it may not be to people 'generally', but it could apply to 'many people'. So I would set against that statement one of my own, which does not contradict it, but which supplements the viewpoint in a far more relevant fashion: *there is some evidence which suggests food additives are a significant risk to many people.* How much difference a small change of wording can make.

The dramatic effects of banning all classes of food additives are often cited as the case against their restriction. 'Without any chemical preservatives,' said one spokesman, 'life as we know it could not exist!' That is both naive and dangerous. Of course it would not be 'life as we know it' – it would be life without preservatives. Certainly life could 'exist'. Drying, heat treatment (as in canning), freezing . . . these methods are already used for a large proportion of our daily foodstuffs and could certainly be utilised if chemical preservatives were to be proscribed overnight, or if they had never existed.

With no anti-oxidants, fats would quickly turn rancid and dried milk and potato would be impractical. With no emulsifiers and texture modifiers there would be no margarine or salad cream, and the low-fat products would disappear. With no colourants or flavourings the confectionery industry would disappear. How typical an example this is of the polarisation effect I have described! No one could campaign for the banning of *all* additives, at least if they wished to maintain any kind of rational profile. What we should seek to do is introduce a new principle – the *principle of minimal interference*. That is a long-winded way of describing what I have in mind, so let us call it, for simplicity, *minimalism*. What this means is that we interfere to the smallest extent necessary. It is quite the opposite of the modern vogue. That, by contrast, is to add to food anything you like if it helps the industry along and does not demonstrable harm – which is the wrong way round. The principle of minimal interference holds that you do nothing to food unless it is necessary to confer some actual benefit on the consumer. The conventional approach benefits the industry, and hopefully does little harm to the consumers in the process. My alternative benefits the consumer, and is as fundamental a change in policy as a decision to use a carrot instead of a stick for the donkey. Most additives are probably harmless; but most are unnecessary too. The problems of epidemiological study, compounded by the possible interaction between compounds in our bodies and the question of cumulative action, make it hard to know where we stand with regard to absolute safety. And those who argue that safety can never be absolute, or that many traditional items of diet produce harmful effects of their own, play right into the hands of my argument. If we are already liable to suffer from materials we have traditionally eaten, there is even less sense in adding unnecessarily to that burden. Any additive that is an unnecessary ingredient in our food should be controlled, for it can from time to time turn out to have undesirable effects. Most do not – though we cannot be sure whether that is because they are actually harmless, or because we cannot demonstrate a cause and effect. It is important to realise that a failure to perceive side-effects can be due, not just to their absence, but to our inability to look properly.

The industry responds to this in a correct and logical manner. We cannot object to artificial materials, they say, when we already consume so many traditional substances that are probably just as harmful. Mere 'artificiality' cannot amount to 'undesirability'. It is true that Vitamin C, ascorbic acid, is a chemical of known composition – like salt, sugar or baking soda – and it is exactly the same whether it is synthesised within an orange on a tree, or in an industrial complex. It is all ascorbic acid, and does us just as much good no matter where it originates.

Traditional foods are often involved with stories of damage to health, and that is because many of them were introduced before recorded history and so were never subjected to the kind of testing that would be necessary if they were being introduced today for the first time. Would cigarettes, window-glass, coal-gas or butter pass modern scrutiny for safety in the home if someone invented them now?

But I am disinclined to accept the view that there is no benefit at all in naturally-occurring substances – that is to say, substances that are produced by living organisms in nature – as opposed to new forms of molecule that are synthesised *de novo*. Some people distrust these new arrivals. Industrial spokesmen, by contrast, will have none of that – synthetic or natural, they say, it is all the same. Who is right? My immediate reaction would be to think

40

that a substance which has become incorporated in our culture over thousands of years or with which we have co-existed just may be easier to live with than a new arrival synthesised by ourselves for the first time in recent years. However, a 'reaction' is no basis for an opinion, so we must turn to the published data.

As an example which seems to confirm that view, consider the seven yellow colourants which make up the start of the E-list. One of them is extracted from the plant which produces it. Six of them are manufactured industrially. Four are artificial dyes, synthesised by the chemical industry, whilst three originated from organic sources in nature. Here they are:

1   CURCUMIN – an extract of the turmeric root, usually sold simply as 'turmeric', and the yellow colour of pillau rice. It is also used to give added yellow to margarine and some cheeses. The commercially available turmeric is extracted from the plant root – it is not synthesised in the laboratory.

2   RIBOFLAVIN – this is vitamin B2 produced either by industrial synthesis or by extraction from yeast cultures. It can be formed in the intestine through the action of bacteria, but our principal dietary sources include green vegetables, offal, eggs and milk. It is used to colour cheese.

3   RIBOFLAVIN-5'-PHOSPHATE – a derivative of riboflavin produced by modifying its molecule in the laboratory which is used to colour fruit products.

4   TARTRAZINE – a widely used synthetic dye, this has applications in fruit squashes, yellow fish (like haddock), marzipan, piccalilli and a host of convenience foods, even mayonnaise and mint sauce.

5   QUINOLINE YELLOW – a duller colour than tartrazine, this synthetic dye is utilised in the manufacture of smoked fish and scotch eggs.

6   YELLOW 2G – a new azo dye.

7   SUNSET YELLOW – used in cakes and confectionery, packet sauces and soups, and orange drink.

These are in fact the first colourants listed in the E-number system, to which I return on p 44; curcumin is E100. They provide an interesting selection. (1) is a molecule found in nature and extracted from the plant which makes it. (2) is a naturally-occurring substance which is sometimes synthesised industrially, and sometimes obtained from the yeast in which it forms. (3) is a form of (2) industrially 'engineered' in the laboratory. (4), (5), (6) and (7) are all azo-dyes – formerly known as coal tar dyes – which are unknown in nature and are produced by the organic chemist. We have here a range of sources through the nature-produced, via the semi-synthetic, to the purely artificial. Research findings show that a range of sensitivities have been demonstrated to the azo-dyes. The manifestations can include urticaria, asthma and a kind of hay-fever, with blurring of vision and the development of purplish patches in the skin. People who are sensitive to aspirin are typically at risk, for these symptoms do not occur in most people. Though they are perfectly safe for the majority of consumers, it has to be remembered that – say, for point of argument – one person in 50 still adds up to a million people in the UK or four million in the US.

For the other three dyes, there are no known adverse reactions. They all derive from sources that occur in nature and which mankind has consumed for centuries. There is no difference between a product that is harvested from the land and one that is copied in the laboratory. But in each case there is no evidence of adverse side-effects. There are seven or eight yellow dyes that occur later in the E-list. They derive from naturally-occurring pigments, such as xanthophyll, which gives a yellow colour to fruit, and in these cases too there have never been reports of harm.

Is it possible that this correlation occurs because I have a selected sample? Perhaps so. Let us then look at all the listed food colours in the E-list. There are twice as many dyes of synthetic origins as there are colours from naturally-occurring sources. Of the synthetic compounds, more than 90% have reports of adverse side-effects in some instances. Less than 10% are completely safe*. For the colourants with natural origins, or which are based on them, only 10% have possible side-effects. 90% seem to be safe. This does not mean that synthetically originated compounds are a danger. To the overwhelming bulk of people they are not, as far

*Less than 10% actually means in this context 'only one'. E142, Green S, is the only synthetic dye in the list with no reported side-effects.

as anybody can tell. That is why it is true to say that 'food additives are no major risk to people generally'.

However, the industry cannot persist in saying that 'there is no reason why natural additives should be safe whil artificial ones are unsafe'. Whether there is 'a reason' or not is one thing – but the clear distribution of possible harm, to some people, produced overwhelmingly by the synthetic dyes compared to the largely harmless naturally-occurring compounds shows where the priorities should lie. In practice they do not reflect reality. The great predominance of synthetically-originated dyes in our food shows how the manufacturers are very keen to use them. The minimum interference principle shows how this could be changed. A 'Minimalist' would argue that:

- no colourants should be used unless they are necessary to make food acceptable – they should never be used merely to slightly modify an already acceptable colour;
- no colourant should be used if it poses a possible hazard to the consumer, if an innocuous alternative exists.

And how do I respond to the manufacturers who insist that the additives are no worse than the foods they go into? You could debate the answer – but it seems to be the wrong question. Minimal interference means that we leave well alone if we can. No matter how large or small the proportion of adverse reactions, there is no virtue in adding to our intake unnecessarily. Suppose that traditional foods and the new additives *all* have an incidence of adverse reactions in – what, 10%?– of cases, then the introduction of 3,000 additives provides 300 new sources of health hazard to mankind, whereas the introduction of none at all would leave us with the burdens we evolved with. Somewhere between the two lies an optimum, 'minimalist' level – where the additives are reducing the health hazards posed by oxidation and rancidity, where they control microbial food poisoning and maintain freshness, but where they do not intrude on the acceptable colours and textures of foods which are in any event perfectly appetising and safe as they are.

A good illustration of the principle already at work, in some ways, is the distinction between 'drink' and 'juice'. A fruit drink can contain almost anything from the list – synergists, anti-foaming agents, flavourings, colourants, antioxidant – and it is normal for

43

a 'drink' to contain nothing at all from a fruit. The product known as *juice*, in contrast, is strictly controlled with minimal interference in mind. Vitamin C can be added to replenish losses during storage (vitamin C is a powerful antioxidant, so it works on both counts). A little sugar can be added if the fruit lacks its own, but the maximum permitted level is 15 grams (½ ounce) per litre – less than 2%. That is all which is permitted in most fruit juice. Fruit acids can be added to apple, grape or pineapple juice to correct the flavour, and an anti-foaming agent is permitted in pineapple juice as a processing aid when necessary. This seems to be the ideal way to use additives – they are being applied to making the product as wholesome and appetising as possible. There would be much public support, I do not doubt, for the idea to catch on throughout the food business. Look at British cheese, as an example – though one preservative is permitted (E201, sodium sorbate) it is never used in the UK. And the colourants used are all plant extracts, such as carotene and annatto (E160a and E160b). This growing campaign has even affected supermarket chains, several of which are now stocking lines that are deliberately selected for their low additive content, or for a shift in favour of natural extracts with a proven track record.

The categorisation of additives in the E-number scheme has not been as successful as it is popular to imagine. This is for several reasons. Firstly, of the 3,000 and more additives in use, only a tenth are approved for use in the UK. Of the total, half are purely cosmetic additives, less than 2% being preservatives. Many of the additives in use are not covered by the scheme. Thus, though colourants are included, flavourings are left out. A further difficulty is posed by the way the numbers are drawn up. There is no self-evident code that the consumer can break. Suppose that all plant pigments were A-, azo-dyes were B-, emulsifiers were C- . . . and so forth. Then, at a glance, you could eliminate foods with a category of additive you wished to avoid. As it is you would need a book in one hand to do the job properly. As a partial answer to the problem, here is a table which lists the main numbers you may need to identify in a hurry. The table is credit-card size, and you should carry a photocopy of it in your wallet or purse. It is not usual for an author to sanction readers copying portions of a book, and the advice does not extend to the making of multiple copies for people who ought to buy the book themselves . . . but a handy pocket-sized list is a very useful way to tackle this problem and I hope it helps.

Handy Guide to E-Numbers

a) No reported side-effects

100–101	282–283	363	460–495
140–142	290	370	501
160–163	296–297	380–381	504–507
170–173	300–304	401–406	509
175	306–309	410	515–516
180	322	415–416	518
201–203	326–327	432–436	526–543
233–234	331–332	440	551–620
260	335–341	442	623–627
262–263	350–353	450	636–920
280	355	450a	927

b) Possible involvement in hyperactivity or allergy

102	122–124	210–220	627
104	127–128	250–251	631
107	132–133	310–312	635
110	150–151	320–321	
120	154–155	621–623	

NOTE: Not all these numbers have been approved as 'E-numbers', though they are in widespread use.

There may be a reason behind the confused way the numbers are currently coded. E-numbers are excellent for the bureaucrats. Such people thrive on numbers and, since obscurity implies the employment of experts to explain what is going on, they could be said to thrive on obscurantism. The confusion certainly aids the industry. By giving all additives a similar-looking E-number, then innocuous natural ingredients (like chlorophyll) acquire a coded appearance that is at first glance indistinguishable from an additive, like phosphoric acid (E140 and E338 respectively). The use of a random coding system with no easy mnemonic makes it harder for people to diagnose what a food contains – most people won't carry a book around with them – and if a categorising system were used, like the one I have proposed here, then it would be much easier for the consumer to reject foodstuffs that contained a specific group of additives (like any azo-dye). So for the industry too, the fact that the lists are incomplete and confusing acts as a buffer against public reaction. However, the public are becoming increasingly aware of the need for high standards of food safety and it is only sensible for the industry to understand that the market is led by consumer demand. Were there to be a new line of food products that were 'azo-dye free' then I have no doubt it would attract an approving sector of the public with commercial benefits to the producer and social benefits for the consumer.

Allergic reactions apart, what of behavioural abnormalities? There is a school of thought that azo-dyes and molecules that are related chemically to aspirin may induce hyperactivity in children.

We have seen how a similar belief about sugar has been widely publicised on the slenderest of evidence as a means of controlling antisocial behaviour in children. The restriction of additives to control hyperactivity has become known, after its inventor, as the Feingold diet. It is important to realise that Ben Feingold has set out to show parents of such children how to recognise what is causing the problems. His approach, as I understand it, does not consist of avoiding all additives for life. What he proposes is that foods containing synthetic colourants or flavours are kept out of the diet, together with any food which contains salicyclates (including many fruits which produce them naturally).

After a month, the 'suspect' foods are then re-introduced into the diet one at a time in an attempt to see which ones are causing problems. The advantage of this approach seems to be that the parents have a chance to perform complex sensitivity tests themselves, and to work out on the basis of home experimentation how to avoid the foods their children cannot tolerate. This saves investigation time, it saves medical costs, and it enables a more detailed investigation to go on with the parents themselves organising it – often a more satisfying way of knowing a job has been done thoroughly and to the client's satisfaction.

Yet when a parent is satisfied that there has been an improvement, is it because of a direct 'pharmacological' effect or could it be due to the parallel causality I proposed earlier? We already know how powerful is the *placebo effect** and that is brought about by the relatively slight revelation that a pill or a potion should be doing you good. So if we have a state of affairs when a patient perceives that a high degree of attention is suddenly being paid to

*The 'placebo effect' interferes with the trial of new medicines if the patient, or even the nurse in charge, knows which pill is supposed to be the inert comparison (the placebo) and which is the active preparation. The effect results from the subconscious transmission to the patient of the fact that the active preparation really *is* supposed to do them good. For this reason, such trials are carried out *double blind* – i.e. the tablets are in numbered containers and the nurse who adminsters them is not aware which is which. The placebo effect is powerful, and can mask the pharmacological effects of drugs. To the medical scientist, that is why it has to be eliminated. To me, it would also be a good reason to harness the effect. If we are truly saying that a belief in a tablet can produce an effect much the same as an actual drug, we should be using the principle rather than eliminating it from our research.

46

them – a far greater change than the taking of a tablet, for this involves a wholesale commitment of people in a caring capacity – it is perfectly possible that this new attitude of care and commitment produces the behavioural improvement.

There have been some trials of the Feingold method carried out by more detached means, and they do not suggest that it works. Esther Wender, a Professor at Salt Lake City, Utah, surveyed thirteen of these trials and noted that almost all of them reported no improvement. In two cases where there was said to be a change for the better, it turned out to have been observed by a parent but was not recorded by any other observers. In conclusion we could say:

a)   food additives are used far too widely, indeed the industry is addicted to them;

b)   many of them are known to produce side-effects in susceptible consumers;

c)   the case against them causing behavioural abnormalities in children is not generally substantiated;

d)   a doctrine of minimal interference, minimalism, would enable us to offer a more realistic set of criteria for the food of the future.

So much for the synthesised compounds used as additives, but what of the traditional agents? Some of those are known to produce ill-health and there is no public reaction against them. One example is the use of nitrates and nitrites to preserve meats. Potassium nitrate is saltpetre, whilst the sodium salt is known as Chile saltpetre (since that is where it was mined). Saltpetre has been used to cure meat for thousands of years. It acts by preventing the multiplication of the bacteria which will otherwise render the food uneatable. The preserved meat can be stored for a prolonged period, an important benefit in primitive societies. But saltpetre can irritate the intestine and produce pain. Irregularities of the pulse have been reported, along with dizziness and muscle weakness. In the body the saltpetre becomes converted from the nitrate to nitrite, which can combine with the haemoglobin of the blood and reduce its oxygen-carrying capacity.

In extreme cases of sensitivity, or sheer overdose, the effects can be more severe: shortness of breath, lowering blood pressure, even circulatory collapse may ensue. Many forms of meat preservation involve the use of nitrates and nitrites, including slicing sausages (like salami); and, as the ultimate fate in the body of nitrate is its conversion to the more harmful nitrite, it is clear that large amounts of these preserved meats could constitute a health hazard. In the intestine the nitrites can be further metabolised to form nitrosamines, and these have been shown to be capable of causing cancer.

Listed in that way these effects become a litany of disasters – from interfering with oxygen transport, to gut cancer, it is an impressive array of potentially serious diseases. Why then have nitrates and nitrites been used? Because they have, for many centuries, been responsible for the *saving* of countless lives. The benefits of using saltpetre in meat greatly outweigh the disadvantages. Particularly in primitive times, when knowledge of foods did not extend to making a vegetarian diet fully nourishing at all, and when northern latitudes needed a supply of food during the long dark days of winter, meat was an important aid for physical development. It is rich in proteins, some vitamins and the fats that are necessary for the maintenance of healthy bodies. And it is because of this fact that *Homo sapiens* is not the only form of life that likes to metabolise meat. Many other organisms too, including bacteria, will do so first, given the chance.

Some of these produce a distasteful product. Others damage the meat so that it cannot be eaten. Some produce toxins that are lethal even in small amounts. Most important of this last group is the relative of the tetanus organism, *Clostridium botulinum*, whose toxin, botulin, is the most intensely poisonous bacterial toxin known. A couple of kilograms would be enough if evenly distributed to wipe out the entire human population of the planet. The disease produced by the toxin is *botulism*, and it manifests itself through interference with the body's transmission of nerve impulses. Botulism is a lethal disease, with paralysis of the muscles and a cessation of breathing; and even a slight contamination of meat with *Cl. botulinum* can kill.

It was long ago found that the soaking of meat in a solution of saltpetre prevents these organisms from growing. Micro-organisms cannot reproduce in a medium rich in nitrates or nitrites, and so the disease risk is immediately eliminated. Little wonder the meat is said to be 'cured' in the process.

The use of this technique over the centuries has been instrumental in saving human life on a huge scale, and the range of cured meat products we have inherited is testimony to an age-old means of preserving food which gave us a range of interesting tastes and textures to delight the palate. It is not enough to say that the health hazards should lead to a ban on these products. That would lead to the withdrawal of a range of traditional meats which people enjoy, and which they are entitled to continue to enjoy if they so wish. Proscription is not the answer: rather, we need to be aware of the background to the preservation and curing of meat and to be alert to the possible drawbacks the process brings with it. If too much salami has been causing you a problem, eat less of it. The need for good oxygen transport in young children has already led to the sensible restriction of these salts in the preparation of food for babies, and clearly a mound of salami sandwiches might not be an appropriate meal for them. If cured meats eaten almost to the exclusion of everything else cause you to have shortness of breath or dizzy spells, then dietary adjustment is the answer. Bans, campaigns and panic are not. What concerns me greatly is that our polarised society leads to the risk that either people will be eating foods that harm them, in complete ignorance of what the risks really are, or that some fashionable campaign will cause heedless worry and stress and lead to a ban on foods that the campaigners do not like (even if the consumer has different views). Many people at this moment may be suffering ill-health because of dietary ignorance, and in a case like that of the cured meats it is vitally important to balance one's gastronomic preferences with the expediency that comes from insight.

We do need a soundly-based sense of objectivity when looking at the question of food additives. It is an appalling prospect that lead used to be employed to make meat redder in an earlier age, yes; but at the time there was not the knowledge of the dangers of lead poisoning that we have today. Current practice allows us to add iron oxides to fish paste, or titanium oxide to horseradish sauce, and I have no doubt both are perfectly innocuous substances. But the principles are similar, and in all instances we are limited not just by our failure to know what the truth really is, but by our ability to know how to look. Our mushrooming consumption of breakfast cereals is an example. They are marketed with proud assertions that they are reinforced with 'one-sixth your daily requirement' of this vitamin or that, which is unhelpful to someone whose diet is already rich enough as it is, and they are

49

targeted by shrewd advertising executives at athletic young people – muscled young executives wrestling with the Porsche en route to the office, strapping young mothers full of vigour and bounce with a vacuum cleaner in one hand and a clutch of babies in the other. Yet what are they getting that is so 'healthy'? A highly processed cereal product, fortified not only with vitamins but with a range of other additives that are neither particularly necessary, nor notably healthy; and the principal ingredients are carbohydrates like starch and sugar. To the devotee of this diet it is perfectly normal to munch these concoctions by the spoonful, whilst dispensing artificial sweeteners into a cup of milky tea . . . to me it is absurd.

We are led astray by our adherence to an unreasoned belief. Views become extreme, and facts quoted to support any given standpoint acquire the diamond-hard certainty of tenets of faith, rather than being – as they more honestly are – data on which to construct an acceptable working hypothesis. So we have those who insist that additives are wonderful and will not hear a word against them. Indeed I know of one senior research scientist in the field who always eats white bread even when his family prefer the health-food alternative, just so that he can celebrate the new era of hi-tech eating. Such people claim any campaign against excess is 'a hoax'. On the other side are those who avoid anything that looks like an additive at thirty paces. I had a breakfast meeting with one of them recently. You might allow me to say how well he fitted the bill. Just as the proponents of food additives seem so often to have a steely look, threatening eyebrows and a manner of aloof and detached superiority, he was the archetypal 'food freak' with metal-rimmed glasses, a straggling beard, thinning hair and a reedy voice. He introduced me to a healthy-eating restaurant where food additives were extirpated at source. He told me, rightly, that this was to be the first time I had ever eaten food that was guaranteed free from all additive chemicals, in a British restaurant. As we talked he listed his fears about the additive menace and what it was doing to a generation for tomorrow, until I could clearly see the reasons which made him want to avoid them at all costs.

And what were we offered for that health-food meal? Why, wholemeal waffles or muffins with fresh farmhouse butter, pure honey or genuine unadulterated maple syrup. A substratum of carbohydrate-rich dough, heavy in gluten, to which so many people prove to be allergic, surmounted by a glutinous topping of saturated animal fat (possibly tainted with the products of rancidity to which I referred earlier) and topped with sugary spreads which have been linked to everything from tooth decay and coronary artery disease to obesity and even cancer. As it happens, I do not believe that sugar is actually as dangerous as many people make out, and I am not convinced that the butter in that case was anything other than fresh and pure as only butter can be . . . always bearing in mind its content of animal lipids. But that is not the point at issue. There is a body of evidence that would recommend you to cut down on such fats, reduce your intake of sugars, moderate your excessive indulgence in carbohydrate, and in some instances curb your intake of gluten. There is certainly a weightier body of evidence against the breakfast I was being offered as there is against the additives he was so strenuously avoiding. So I declined the kind offer of food, and took a little juice and some fresh fruit instead.

CHAPTER FOUR

There are extraneous substances in our food which are not additives at all, but contaminants. That is, they are there by accident, left over from some other activity. There are hormones in meat, metals contaminating vegetables, pesticide residues in fruit. For these the controls are lax, even non-existent. The hazards they pose may prove to be among the more serious that face us in an era of intensive farming production.

There can be no doubt that we need to control pests by artificial means. Pests evolved to survive by spreading from one plant to another under trying circumstances, since in nature the host plants are usually scattered about amongst a huge variety of other species in which the pest is less interested. A species of insect that has solved the problem of survival in such difficult circumstances finds it extraordinarily easy to pass along a row of crops growing in intimate proximity.

Some species of pest (like the aphids) have even evolved parthenogenetic reproduction – i.e. virgin birth without the intervention of a male – so that isolated individuals can reproduce fast enough to survive. Our desire to grow plants intensively, on farms that feed us, means that we are raising crops in a profoundly unnatural state. But this is only to be expected: as civilised human beings we are living in a totally unnatural set of circumstances and we need unnatural means to keep alive at all.

There are many ways in which pests can be controlled. One of these relies on the use of biological predators, species that actually feed on the pest and in this way keep it under control. The species can be another insect, or it can even be a bacterium or a virus that spreads amongst the pest and wipes it out. Another possibility is the use of chemicals that control the pests. These are the most widely used form of pesticide, and it is the residues of these chemicals that are now being found in our food.

The amount of pesticides that are sold suggests that the industry has acquired its own momentum, just as has happened in the food additive industry. Ten years ago British pesticide sales were running around £80 million. In the mid–1980s the figure has topped £350 million and now some 30 million kg of pesticide chemicals are added to crops. There is no legal restriction on pesticides, only guidelines issued by the EEC and the WHO. Some laws have been passed in Britain to control the use of pesticides, but there is still no limit on the amount of pesticides that can be used, or the number of times crops should be sprayed. The main safeguards we have are the tests carried out by the Public Health analysts – but in an age of cutbacks there is likely to be less testing unless public pressure causes it to increase.

Their tests suggest that one-third of the fruit and vegetables we eat have some pesticide contamination, whilst one in ten fruit samples, together with one in five vegetables, contains more than the reporting levels set by the government. It is suggested that farmers can control pests in organically-grown crops by more natural means, and it has been claimed that they do not cost more than the pesticide-treated version. That is hard to sustain; most of the data available show that the costs are actually some 30% higher. But here too we run into the polarisation of views. The proponents of pesticides say they are harmless when properly utilised and should be available to farmers, whilst their opponents insist that nature knows best and that all pesticides should be banned. There is in this case too a sound basis for the use of the safer pesticides in the spirit of minimal interference – i.e. to protect crops when they need it, and not to saturate every growing thing just in case the need arises later on.

Campaigns against pesticides can rebound. The use of DDT, for instance, led to an astonishing reduction in the levels of malaria in the tropics. Before the Second World War the levels in India were in the hundreds of thousands, whilst in the 1950s they were down to a few tens of thousands of cases. The banning of DDT, which was used to control the malaria mosquito, has directly

53

caused the levels to rise again until there are many times more victims now than there were decades ago. Yet DDT has a very good safety record in human terms – it caused damage to the eggs of birds of prey, certainly, but it did not cause damage to people; whereas its banning certainly has caused a massive amount of morbidity and death. The problem with DDT is its persistence. It still occurs in vegetable and fruit analyses to this day, sometimes because it is being used illicitly but often because it is persisting in the soil. The long-term effects of pesticide residues in food are difficult to calculate. In massive populations we will probably need them unless we are to starve a future generation, but any over-use is likely to expose us to a level of risk that should be unacceptable.

Short-term risks are easier to detect when the spraying gets out of hand. People are sometimes sprayed as well as the crops. The spraying of a party of firemen with pesticides had seven kept in hospital for twenty-four hours, complaining of stinging eyes and difficulty in breathing. In other cases the skin of people accidentally sprayed has been affected by eczema and even blistering and each year in Britain there may be a couple of hundred complaints sent in to the Civil Aviation Authority. However, there are more cases than that: most people have never heard of the Civil Aviation Authority and would not know where to lodge a complaint, and in addition many of the people affected live in local communities in which a written complaint against a local farmer would not be very popular. But, if the hard selling of pesticides continues and they are used more than is strictly necessary, then cases of this sort can only increase.

Heavy metals are a problem that usually affects people from sources other than food – the inhalation of lead from fuel exhaust, for example. Yet there are signs that we may be allowing amounts of pollution to reach quite high levels. The River Forth in Scotland is currently receiving up to two tonnes of mercury per year from the industrial complex at Grangemouth. Shellfish in the area have been shown to contain more than twenty times the EEC's standard level of mercury contamination of 0.3 parts per million (ppm), and that mercury can make its way up the food chain until it accumulates in the bodies of fish which feed on the smaller creatures of the sea.

The industrial end of this argument points out that the mercury that goes into the river is inorganic, and therefore largely ignored by higher life forms. However, bacteria that live in sea silt can metabolise inorganic mercury into the methylmercury form, which is taken up much more readily. It was this form that led to the Minimata tragedy in Japan, which disabled 100 people through the eating of contaminated seafood and eventually killed 43 of them. Seawater mercury levels in that area were 8 ppm, whilst the current maximum in the Firth of Forth is 6.6 ppm. There is no real comparison so far as danger is concerned, since the Minimata people ate a diet composed principally of contaminated fish from the bay, and this is not the case in Scotland. But it remains a salutary lesson in priorities that such high levels are once again occurring, this time with official sanction, and in an era when millions of pounds have been spent in removing mercury from industrial discharges in Scotland.

Lead is an insidious poison which comes to us in our food as well as in the air we breathe. The EEC level for lead in the bloodstream is 35 micrograms (μg) whilst in Britain the limit is set at 25μg. But there are opinions that hold that even these levels can produce signs and symptoms in people. Most vegetables do not so much accumulate lead from the ground water through their roots, instead they collect it from the air around them and for this reason the problem is most marked in areas near busy roads. The recommended level of lead in green leafy vegetables like cabbages and lettuces is 1 μg per kg for adult consumption, and for children a lower level of 0.2 μg per kg – but samples of lettuces and cabbages often show higher levels than this, at least before they are washed. It is normal these days for unwashed lettuces, for instance, to be above the safety limit recommended for children. Thoroughly washed they typically contain about that level of 0.2 μg/kg. This lead arises from the 10,000 tonnes per year which are poured into the air we breathe from the exhaust fumes of motor vehicles. There are campaigns to have this danger removed, for cars can be designed to run without lead in petrol and the environmental load they impose is hardly reasonable any longer.

Hormones are found in meat when you least expect them. That is because they are often used illegally, in countries which have banned them altogether. Anabolic steroids are used to make meat-producing animals develop heavier bodies, which makes an additional profit for the farmer with minimum financial outlay. The costs are around £2–£10 per animal, and an injection of the steroid will put on extra meat worth to the farmer as much as £50. Anabolic steroids have been (illicitly) used by athletes who wish to short-circuit the effort in gaining extra muscle, and in farming they were used widely in the 1970s. Today, more than half of beef cattle are treated with these growth-promoting agencies. But the current pattern of use has varied from nation to nation: thus they are all banned in Italy, whilst there are no restrictions on the hormones that may be used for fattening cattle in Ireland.

Yet it was in Italy that high levels of stilboestrol were detected in one recent study. The reason was that farmers, determined not to be left without the advantages that farmers had in other countries, were obtaining the drug illegally and injecting it themselves into their own animals. However there is to be an easy and effective answer to this problem, for all growth-promoting steroids are to be banned in future. Starting in 1986, a programme is to be introduced across the EEC to ban all anabolic agents in the fattening of cattle – though Britain has claimed to be a 'special case' and is being allowed to phase them out over a timescale reaching to 1989.

Hormones pose problems because one can never be sure what effects they may have in the long term. The hallmark of a hormone is that a little goes a long way. A dose of a few milligrams of the right hormone can have drastic effects on the consumer. So far there has been scant evidence of any harm resulting from the use of steroids in cattle farming, but one warning shot has been fired from the study of women treated medically with very high levels of di-ethyl stilboestrol many years ago. They were given the drug in a course of therapy during pregnancy, and it was later reported that this has been related to the development of cancer in their daughters after they had in turn reached sexual maturity. This is an extreme manifestation of a drug used in high dosages when the level of understanding was not as great as is now the case – but with precedents like this in mind it is easy to see why the EEC authorities have been persuaded to ban all such agencies from use. The extra cost to the consumer is calculated to be around 4p per lb, though I do not recall consumers being told they were *saving* 4p per lb when the anabolic steroids were at their height . . .

Chemical contaminants are not the only danger in our food, however. The risks from food poisoning are increasing as people are more inclined to rush food preparation and to ignore essential safety measures. There are two main groups of food-poisoning organisms*, one in which the bacteria themselves cause an infection in the patient, and the other where the bacteria produce a toxin in the food *before* it is eaten.

An example of the first category is botulism, to which we have referred, and that is fortunately a rare occurrence. Much more common is the formation of toxins in cream by a growth of *Staphylococcus* bacteria. The staphylococci prefer to grow in conditions which are:

- rather alkaline (they will not grow in an acidic medium below pH 4.5)
- rich in carbohydrates (and, to a lesser extent, proteins)
- kept at near body temperature of 37°C (a range of 30–40°C is acceptable for growth).

A favourite medium which combines the best of all these – from the bacterial viewpoint – is a trifle. Made with sponge and whipped cream, then stood in a warm room for the best part of a day, the staphylococci will rapidly proliferate and liberate a toxin which causes illness in the person who eats it. The effects on the patient are to produce intestinal irritation, so there may be violent cramp-like abdominal pains with blood in faeces or vomit in an extreme case, and headache. Because the toxins are already lying in wait for the unwary, the symptoms appear very soon after the food is eaten – a few hours at the most – but they pass off within twenty-four hours or so.

There are many other organisms which produce toxins in food, of which the most classic example is the ergot produced in infected rye by the fungus *Claviceps purpurea*. Thousands of Soviet soldiers died from eating contaminated rye flour during World War II, and the occurrence of this toxic phenomenon in the rye flour of the Middle Ages has encouraged some historians to think that ergotism could have been a reason why people were so unhealthy at that time. The effects of the toxin are a little like those of LSD,

---

*The term 'food poisoning' is open to misinterpretation, for it is not the same thing at all as food being contaminated by some external poison. The term 'food poisoning' anachronistically refers to the contamination of foodstuffs by bacteria which cause an illness in the consumer. If a better term occurs to you then let me know – it is time we improved on the standard phrase.

and it seems possible that the celebrated behaviour of the Salem Witches in the USA resulted from their consumption of infected rye bread.

It is a relative of the botulism organism, *Clostridium perfringens*, which gave rise to one of the most widespread forms of food poisoning. The organism has very resistant spores which can withstand cooking temperatures around 100°C, but which germinate as the cooked food approaches body heat as it cools. The typical pattern is that contaminated meat is roasted, though not well roasted, and is then allowed to stand in a warm place for several hours. The bacteria hatch out from their spores (having survived the cooking) and grow inside the meat where they liberate their toxic by-product. Here too the symptoms come on within an hour or two of consumption, and rarely last longer than twenty-four hours. The principal result of ingesting *Cl perfringens* toxin is cramp and diarrhoea and the aching symptoms of a twenty-four hour influenza. The condition is commoner in the USA than in the United Kingdom, largely because meat is served rare in the US, and is more often traditionally well done in the UK.

Such episodes are often missed, and are rarely reported to a doctor, unless they occur in unusual circumstances, such as the episode in 1975 on a flight from Anchorage, Alaska, to Denmark. The bacteria were *Staphylococcus aureus* from an infected cut on the chef's hand, and the meal he was making for the passengers was ham and scrambled eggs. The completed meals were left standing in sealed containers for about six hours prior to take off and on this occasion they remained near body temperature the whole time. It was an ideal situation for the organisms to grow and over 150 people became violently ill with severe cramps and diarrhoea with vomiting. The plane by then was high over the Arctic with nowhere to set down and the scenes aboard – with 150 people stricken with diarrhoea and only a few toilets on board – were extremely difficult. In the event, everyone recovered within a day or two just as you would expect, though the head chef of the airline was so upset by the episode that he reputedly committed suicide.

The second category of food poisoning organisms is the group that actually infect the human host. The classic organism in this category is *Salmonella*, of which there are several species. The most notorious of these is *S typhi*, which causes typhoid fever, whilst the others cause paratyphoid in its various forms. The particular danger of *S typhi* is the fact that only a few organisms are enough

58

to cause the infection in the host, whilst for the other species of *Salmonella* the inoculum is greater – perhaps a dose of thousands of the bacteria, compared with just a few dozen for typhoid. This is why typhoid is so infectious. *Staphylococcus* can infect the human host – it is these bacteria which cause spots, boils and septicaemia – but when they are eaten in an infected trifle the organisms are killed by the acid in the stomach. The toxins they leave behind do the damage. The salmonella organisms resist the stomach acid and grow in the intestine, and for this reason the symptoms take longer to occur. This form of food poisoning may appear in the range of 7–72 hours from ingestion. It also lasts longer, for forty-eight hours in many cases, and severe dehydration can set in if the patient is young, elderly or debilitated. Watery stools are produced and there may be vomiting. D & V (diarrhoea and vomiting, in medical shorthand) is often due to salmonelliasis of this sort.

Cases of food poisoning are no longer rare, and they seem to occur with disturbing (perhaps increasing) frequency in places where you would hope they might be avoided – like hospitals. We have seen how you can regulate your intake of additives, should you so desire, by reading the labels and opting for the pure alternative; and how metals on the dust coating leafy vegetables can be reduced by the simple expedient of washing them before consumption. There are similarly easy ways of avoiding bacterial food poisoning. The bacteria, whether *Staphylococcus* or *Salmonella*, need a warm environment in which to proliferate. They also need to get into the food in the first place. So there are two principles on which hygiene can be based:

1   Keep bacteria away from food. Do not cough onto foods, do not bite fingers, etc., whilst preparing food, and remember to clean hands before handling food. In institutional circumstances (as in the hospital kitchen) watch for infected personnel. For mass handling, sterile plastic gloves would be a help, though that would be unnecessary at home.

2   Keep food very hot, or very cold. Avoid prolonged periods at body temperature. This is what really causes problems. Food that is cooked should go quickly to its cooking temperature, and should be allowed to cool rapidly afterwards, if it is not being eaten straightaway. Make the trifle late in the day; or if that is impossible make sure it is kept refrigerated meanwhile. Cook the meat

thoroughly and serve it at once; if that is not possible then cool it down and keep it in the fridge.

Additives, external contaminants, bacteria; all are targets of concern and all can be controlled by individual action. I have said how the worry and fear of what is in food only adds to the burden of distress which people suffer, and to our 'tension load'. An answer to the problems is what people need to have, and in all these cases there is much that can be done – as an individual – to react positively to your food, rather than to retreat, stressful, from the supposed threats it poses.

Food is there to be enjoyed. Personal freedom and the ability to alter your destiny are what prevent the burden of frustration and stress. Through understanding comes freedom, and when it can be allied to a programme of action the effect is greatest. Almost exhilarating, in fact.

CHAPTER FIVE

Proteins are what life is all about. Proteins make up the protoplasm – the cytoplasm – which lives. They are also the most complex chemical substances known to us. The formula for a simple sugar, like glucose, is $C_6H_{12}O_6$ and it has a molecular weight of 180 (i.e. each molecule weighs 180 times as much as a single atom of hydrogen). But if you look at a relatively simple protein it has a molecular weight measured in the tens of thousands, and a correspondingly complex formula. Lactoglobulin, for instance, found in milk, has a formula which is (probably):

$$C_{1864}H_{3012}O_{576}N_{468}S_{21}$$

Many other proteins have a molecular weight up in the millions, and it would be difficult to see how we could accurately ascertain their exact formula.

What does protein *look* like? The familiar example is egg white, a glutinous, slimy and viscous semi-transparent material. This is a typical form of protein, and the bodily secretions are, in the main, protein solutions. Living cells are composed most importantly of protein. There are other components too, such as the structural elements and energy-store centres, but it is the protein which is the 'living' part of the cell. From this there follow two important conclusions:

a) an adequate supply of materials which can make protein is important in any healthy diet;

61

b) food composed of cells will be rich in protein.

These facts make scientific opinion value protein very highly in the diet, and rightly so; without proteins you will die. On the other hand, you do not require a very large amount of protein – roughly an ounce a day will suffice, if it is the right kind of protein. As a result, this issue has experienced those great swings in fashion: a generation ago we all had to eat as much high-protein food as we could, now the need is perceived as being less – until some current publications show a swing in opinion that is so extreme, that they ridicule the earlier views altogether and almost make protein-eating seem unpleasant and, at best, a necessary evil. Once again we have a polarisation of views, rather than a sensible and realistic synthesis of current knowledge.

There was one important misunderstanding in the past, and that was to insist that only *meat* protein was suitable to ensure healthy growth. Nowadays that view is scorned, but it was not held for ill-considered reasons. As I have explained, it is meat that is made up of cells and the cells are clearly rich in the very kind of protein that you need to make meat. Therefore (and it is a very sensible conclusion in many ways) plenty of meat in the diet will mean plenty of new cells made in the eater.

Two items of knowledge show that the view was not as sound as it seems. Firstly, meat is not all the same in terms of its value to human eaters. Eggs and fish are both better sources of protein, if that is all we consider, than beef. Secondly, the assumption that proteins were somehow inevitably poor if they came from vegetable sources was incomplete. It is true that the best balance of the building-blocks from which proteins are assembled comes from animal sources, but plants contain a good supply too if they are chosen correctly.

Proteins are assembled from sub-units known as amino acids. They are items in the kit. If a few are missing then you cannot make the finished article, no matter how many of the others you may have. The amino acids that are essential in mankind are these:

Leucine	Phenylalanine
Isoleucine	Threonine
Lysine	Tryptophan
Methionine	Valine

In addition:
Histidine (under investigation as possibly essential)
Arginine (essential for infants).
There are many other amino acids that the body uses to manufacture proteins, but these can all be made in the body. The ten or so in the list above cannot be manufactured by human metabolism, and so they must be present in the diet. Clearly, the eating of some meat in the daily food intake is an important source of these, since they all occur in the proteins of other animals. The old-fashioned view that meat is a useful item of the diet remains entirely valid. As we have seen, there are many ways of looking at vegetarianism (p 28 *et seq*) but it remains true that meat does provide an important range of amino acids which we do require in our daily diet.

There are many amino acids in the proteins from plants. The reason these have been held to be somehow 'inferior' is because the complete spectrum is not present in proteins from a single plant. Thus, the protein from corn contains very low amounts of tryptophan; soy bean protein shows too little methionine. This means that a person eating either food as a source of protein would be unable to utilise the other amino acids effectively. They are all necessary, so if there is only ten percent of one constituent in the protein you are eating, then you will only be able to utilise about ten percent of *all* the amino acids, meaning you would metabolically ignore the ninety percent of the others that are there in abundance. It is for this reason that meat proteins were always known as 'first class proteins' by nutritionists, whilst plant proteins were dubbed 'second class'.

The error in this model is that it assumes that soy, or corn, is going to be your only source of protein. But suppose your diet contained both versions, what would be the result? Your diet would then be adequately supplied with both amino acids, since corn contains two-thirds as much methionine as egg protein (which would therefore mean that the deficiency of soy in that amino acid would be rectified) whilst soy contains ninety percent as much tryptophan as does egg. So, if the two were eaten together, the protein balance would be restored. In cereal crops it is lysine which is most usually reduced. In corn protein, it is present in an amount that is roughly equivalent to 45% of the levels in egg; in other cereals it can be very much less. That means cereals would be a poor source of amino acids, the proportion being taken up by the body being limited by the low level of lysine.

However, pulses – beans and peas – often contain very high levels of lysine. So this means that, if a diet that contains cereals and pulses is eaten, the result is that the two deficiencies cancel each other out and the diet becomes healthily balanced once more. I tend to have a marked respect for the traditions which we have culturally built up over centuries, and it is very interesting how our traditions and our instinct combine to give us a taste for exactly this kind of balance. In India you find the chapatis eaten with dhall (cereal- and pulse-originated); in the Middle East you find a similar balance between pitta and hummus (again, cereal and pulse). Even in our own more recent times we have seen an instinctive linking for another nutritionally-correct blend of cereal product with a topping of cooked pulses. It is called baked beans on toast.

This has led to a change in attitudes towards protein. Suddenly, meat is no longer always necessary; suddenly, eating meat is a bad thing to do. It is even said that meat promotes lust and damages the kidneys. So here, too, within a generation we have seen a dramatic change in polarity which can only unsettle and confuse the public. Where is the truth? To begin with, let us settle the protein-and-lust theory. It dates from the 1880s, when the keepers at the London Zoo were troubled by aggressive and uncontrollable bears in the bear-pit. A change of diet was instituted, the bears being given bread instead of their normal diet of meat. Bread is a useful item of diet, because it has a fairly good balance of amino acids. Like other cereal derivatives it is made with flour that is low in lysine, but bread is made with milk and yeast which both contain lysine, and so the balance is largely restored. Even so, there is a lot less protein in bread than there is in meat, and the result in the London Zoo experiments was very clear. The bears became docile, meek, quiet; their listless compliance was in marked contrast to their aggressive and 'lustful' manner beforehand. The conclusion drawn was that the meat – and all its protein – made them so aggressive. Cut down the protein so that their bodies became less liable to the 'assault' it entailed on their delicate inner workings, and they reverted to behaviour that was more compatible with what the keepers expected. For one thing, it made them much easier to handle.

This case was published in the literature of science and since acquired a folkloric popularity in the field. To this day there are men with street posters parading about and insisting that protein causes lust, and meat makes the animal organism dangerously aggressive. Yet there was another explanation for the bears' behaviour. It was not that the meat made them aggressive at all; it was their nature and the conditions in which they were constrained to live that had produced that entirely natural effect. The reason the change of diet made them compliant and gentle was because they were being starved of vitally important nutriments. Of course they were quiet: they had no energy with which to be anything else. I have known of human vegetarians who find themselves calmer, gentle and listless compared to their earlier meat-eating form, and who interpret that as a change of character. In some cases that might be so – a person who discovers a level of humanity they did not earlier realise, and who gives up meat eating as a personal rejection of the cruelties of animal farming, may well become a much nicer person as a result.

But in some other cases I wonder whether the timid nature one sees is the result of malnutrition. A vegetarian (and even more so a vegan) needs careful instruction and advice on obtaining a balanced dietary input. Sometimes people simply give up meat from their daily diet, and what is worse inflict that on their children. Infants need a very high level of protein for their development to proceed, and brain development can be stunted if an infant receives an ineffective diet. There are instances of strange little babies who turn up at clinics and hover near the base-line of normal development, who later turn out to have received a diet largely made up of commercial baby food containing starch and fruit pulp, and little else. What they need is some animal protein, and they need it as a matter of urgency. A little scrambled egg, for example, would be ideal; so too would fish. Yet fish remains an unacceptable item of diet for a great number of people. The view may stem from the tradition that fish was easy to digest and so was a suitable food for invalids. I have shown how people often act in a way that is subconsciously designed to protect against illness and it could be that the traditional working-class disinclination to eat fish derives from the association between convalescents and a fish diet. If so it is time that changed, for fish would be a very valuable source of protein for infants.

The dangerous distortions that result from the swings in opinion are exemplified by a condition known as *kwashiorkor* in the tropics.

65

It is often found in newly-weaned babies and infants whilst the mother is breast-feeding the new arrival in the family (and the word actually means something like 'the illness that afflicts the firstborn whilst the young child is being breast-fed'). It is a specific syndrome, in which infants have thin arms and legs, prominent eyes and a hugely distended stomach. The hair falls out; the skin becomes a purplish colour. It is a complex disease, and my private instincts are to believe that the real cause has not yet been found. There is no sign yet that there is a 'kwashiorkor virus', but the models that have been put forward for it are not a completely satisfactory explanation of this haunting and dangerous disease.

But one of the most popular hypotheses to account for it was that kwashiorkor was due to a lack of protein. This has become the most widespread thesis. It holds that the baby receives a diet with roughly enough energy, but with too little protein to sustain the bodily development on which its survival depends. At the time when protein was highly fashionable and one of the 'good guys' of the field, this view was generally accepted by nutritionists. In more recent years there have been so many exceptions to the predictable rules that it has become plain that the disease is more complex than that, in all probability, and the real cause has yet to emerge. However, the anti-protein fad has gone much further than this. In the words of one recently published study, which I have para-phrased for clarity, kwashiorkor does not result from protein deficiency at all; it results from a lack of *food*.

This trendiness is dangerous. It oversimplifies the issues. Kwashiorkor is not due to a lack of food, as such, at all. Such a condition is well known and is a quite different syndrome known as *marasmus*. Here you see children who are tiny, weak and thin, and who are simply starved. But kwashiorkor itself is a different matter, a distinct disease if you like, and it is not good enough to blur the lines between diseases that have been intensively studied for decades and fashionably trumpet the view that protein shortage cannot be the cause. In all probability, it is in some way involved. The chances are, on the basis of our current knowledge, that victims of the disease could be given some extra protein, the equi-valent of an egg every day or two, or the addition of some animal protein to their diet. Alternatively, a supplement based on selected pulses or wheats could help rectify the missing amino acids. It may be that the symptoms of diseases like kwashiorkor could be related to a lack of a specific amino acid in the diet. If a cause of that kind were to be discovered then we would have an easily recognisable way of finding and providing a tailor-made solution to an otherwise intractable difficulty. Meanwhile, the trendy opinion that throws protein into disfavour must not be allowed to extend to misleading people over the cause of some of nature's most debilitating conditions.

How much protein (of good quality) do we really need? The smallest amount we see in communities that seem well nourished is about 30 grams (an ounce). This is the amount fed to patients on dialysis machines, sufferers from kidney malfunction, who need to excrete the smallest possible amount of surplus. Most authorities aim rather above the minimum requirement, and it is perfectly correct that they do. Nobody should balance on the edge of minima: if the minimum temperature at which you can exist is known, or the minimum amount of oxygen in the air, then there is no benefit in teetering on that balance. The minimum is simply that – an amount below which you should not go. Being rather above it is fine, for the extra protein is metabolised and simply provides a comfortable safety margin. Of the, say, 50g per day that people could sensibly eat, about half should be in the form of eggs, meat or fish, and the rest derived from cereals and pulses. That is for a normally omnivorous diet: corresponding adjustments could be made for diets that lean less heavily on meat as an amino acid source. They would have an added advantage, namely a lowering in the amounts of saturated animal fats that we consume. There is a lot of cholesterol in eggs, for instance, which it might be sensible to limit. I say 'might' because the evidence linking cholesterol in the diet with cholesterol in the bloodstream is not definitive; and anyway you need cholesterol in reasonable amounts in the bloodstream to develop normally. The insulation of the nerve cells and the nerve cords of the body is largely due to cholesterol, and it is also cholesterol on which the architecture of the brain is based. So with none at all you would die.

What about body-building diets? In Western countries people often eat some 100 gm per day – that is roughly three times the absolute minimum – of which more than half comes from meat. Now, suppose you wish to develop a massive physique. Many athletes do. They take a diet that can rate as high in protein as 300 grams of protein a day, often in the form of dozens of eggs and great slabs of beefsteak. With heavy training and intensive exercise they can then put on extra muscle. But let us look at this closely. Take an extra 20lbs of muscle in a month (which would be an unimaginably severe test of body-building, nearly a record I would say). You would need to eat an extra 20lbs of protein to attain this, would you? The answer is – no. Most of the extra muscle is water and fat anyway, and the proportion of dry weight that is protein is only 20%. So the extra you would require would be *four pounds*, that is all. Divide this by the 30 days in a month and you find that all you would need to do would be to eat about 100 grams a day of total protein. That is quite close to what many Western people eat normally.

It is not a great excess of consumption that sets the body on the road to development, it is the exercise you take and the life-style you adopt (the anabolic drugs, if you are determined to get bulky at whatever cost). The body knows exactly where to set its own developmental controls, and extra amounts of protein in the diet will not on their own improve matters, once you are already eating the basic minimum. I am not alone in having raised little boys who sat at the dinner table and ate at least as much as father, yet who remained obstinately smaller than their best friends of the same age, until that magic moment when the body's internal regulatory mechanisms switch into action and the next stage of development is placed in train. Then – almost overnight, it seems – the body enlarges, the muscles spread, the weight increases and the muscles bounce out like inflatable gas-bags on a life-raft. The child is eating as much as before; it is just that the equilibrium point has been reset. So those athletes who eat only protein are doing nothing to supply what the body needs, instead they are greatly increasing the load on the kidneys and the other organs that handle the excess. Eating 300 grams when 30 is enough for survival and 50 is the sign of a good diet places a needless extra loading on the kidneys and, though they would handle the extra without difficulty in normal health, they would be hard put to keep up with it all if some slight kidney malfunction were to become manifest. The fact that the kidneys might begin to react in a sick patient is not a suggestion that we should all keep near the minimum protein requirement, but there are limits. Ten times as much as you need is way over the top.

There is no need to worry about protein levels in a typical Western diet. They are likely to be within the normal range without outside interference, and protein deficiency would be hard to find. It may be that some obese and haggard youngster who consumes nothing but fried potatoes and popcorn may be rather short on protein, but then any parent who allows that kind of thing to go on does not need a chapter in a book like this to point out, judiciously, that the diet is unsatisfactory. Body-builders will also find that there is enough protein in a good Western diet, without spending vast sums on proteins which the body cannot use and which then have to be metabolised and excreted. The lustful and carnal consequences of eating protein are non-existent, even though an aggressive and lustful individual could arguably be quietened down if he ate a deficient diet which caused him to become weak, listless and compliant through under-nutrition.

Some people are allergic to proteins in the diet. Milk in particular is a significant cause of allergic diseases in humans, indeed a significant amount of morbidity is due to undetected allergy to milk proteins in Britain. In the USA there is more awareness of the problem, and so you tend to find over-enthusiastic 'diagnoses' of victims in America and a similar rate of under-diagnosis in the UK. Heat denatures proteins, and so sterilised milk* can produce lower rates of allergy than pasteurised milk. One case of a boy allergic to pasteurised milk is known; he had severe eczema which was proved to be due to an allergy to bovine serum albumen. Sterilised milk, which had been heated to a higher temperature during processing, rid him of the disease. For the same reason, some people who are milk-intolerant can take reconstituted evaporated milk from tins without problems.

Milk is widely seen as a healthy product. In Britain the advertisements stress the vitamins, the proteins, the calcium, all of which is true; though they omit any mention of the saturated animal fats and the commercially idiotic fact that most of milk is water. The weight of water that is trans-shipped in the name of distributing the products of the dairy industry is phenomenal. How much petroleum is consumed in the process of moving it around is anyone's guess – but milk is not a 'natural' food for anyone but a calf and it should be no surprise that the huge amounts we are cajoled into consuming inevitably bring with them the risk of

*The term is a misnomer, since the milk is not actually 'sterilised'. Some spore-forming bacteria can still survive. But UHT milk, which is raised to higher temperatures for a short time, is actually 'sterile' and contains no residual bacteria.

allergy to the proteins they contain. In some people the symptoms can be severe – thus there was a family in which the grandmother had the runny nose prevalent in cases of hay-fever, facial swelling and headaches for most of her life; the mother had headaches, tiredness and a runny nose too; and the son had similar symptoms and was difficult at school. A milk-free diet reportedly controlled the symptoms in a matter of days, but even a trace of milk in a cup of tea for grandmother led to an immediate recurrence of the problems.

Now, most people do not suffer from allergies to milk. For many people it is a pleasant part of one's diet and in sensible amounts makes a perfectly reasonable item of food. Against that we must set the commercial pressures which pay farmers to produce more milk than we normally need, and the fact that society accepts milk as a thoroughly wholesome and desirable food. It only seems that way because the industry carefully censors out any reference to the 'bad side' of milk which, like most foods, is useful in moderate amounts but less so in excess. And in the people who are allergic to milk proteins it can be a real source of problems. Surveys suggest that perhaps 5% of babies develop this form of allergy. Whatever the percentage in adults, it is worth realising that:

a)   For most people milk allergy will never be a problem;

b)   for those that are made ill by it, recognition of the problem can lead to an easy solution.

Goat's milk is no answer to the problem, according to the available research. Allergies to cow's milk are related to intolerance to goat's milk, in people who make the change. Goat's milk has the aura of naturalness about it, but it is important to realise that the goat is not recognised by the agricultural legislators as a milk-producing animal and so it is free from the regulations surrounding dairy cattle. You may breathe a sigh of relief at that, and I share your distrust of heavyweight authoritarian bodies; but the result is that the safety regulations for goat's milk lie only in the mind of the producer. So the levels of contamination are typically higher, and levels of freshness and purity rather lower, than is the case for cow's milk producers.

Perhaps you feel that this talk of allergies is related to our craving for animal products, and that if we were to leave them

70

alone and eat nothing but plant-based foods we would be better off. That cannot be justified. Parallel to the widespread intolerance of milk protein is the allergy to gluten in cereals. This gives rise to coeliac disease, sometimes called non-tropical sprue; a condition in which diarrhoea and the production of fatty faeces appear, and the patient begins to lose weight. What has happened is that the intestinal wall is reacting to the gluten in wheat flour. It becomes smooth and diseased, and the gut is no longer able properly to absorb the food within it. The condition is chronic and can be distressing for the patients and their families. The answer is usually to avoid gluten altogether, which need not mean eating no bakery produce at all, for gluten-free flour is now readily available. The disease can take some months to clear up, and in some people it exists at a low level which is hard to diagnose; this can lead to a long-standing disease in adults which may lie apparently quiescent for prolonged periods.

These are interesting conditions, for they remind us that even the most widely accepted items of our traditionally acceptable diet can in fact produce illness in some people. Both milk and bread allergies appear because a child becomes sensitised to the proteins early in life, so one way to guard against such conditions is to keep the foods away from children when they are very young. There is a fad for giving children cow's milk foods when they are too young for them. Subjecting infants to the challenge of milk proteins from cows when they are intended to be drinking the home-grown article is hazardous.

The use of baby cereal products is similarly unwise when coeliac disease and gluten allergy may be triggered. People believe that the sooner you can have a child weaned, or eating, or potty-trained, or walking, or whatever, then it is heading for an illustrious future. Now it is true that a child can be influenced towards these specific actions earlier than otherwise it might have been. But – and this is the point to which people have yet to awaken – there is no coordination between the age at which a child becomes able to do something for the first time, and the excellence with which it performs as an adult. There is no evidence that a child who writes early is going to become a novelist, or that an early walker will take to dancing or mountaineering. Thrusting false precocity on children is an unhealthy manifestation of the modern era and its emphasis on competitiveness; and when children are taken from the breast and challenged with the alien proteins of grain and

71

cow's milk we are possibly heading for trouble. Infants are only infants once, and it is unnecessary to rush them through the process in the entirely erroneous belief that the result will be a brain surgeon or a band manager with a Rolls Royce in the drive. Parents should not seek to search for their own attainments through the precocity of their children; babies should be babies for as long as they wish and if that means reducing the chances of gluten allergy or milk induced asthma, then so much the better.

CHAPTER SIX

Excess proteins are burned by the body to provide energy. But of course the greatest sources of day-to-day energy in the running of the body chemistry derive from fats and carbohydrates. Fats are the most concentrated source of energy available to the body, roughly ten calories for every gram of fat (say, 300 per ounce) compared with about four calories from carbohydrate (roughly 125 per ounce). Fats are familiar to us. Though protein seems somewhat strange in the sense that it is hard to visualise what protein is actually 'like' (I have attempted to clarify the picture in the previous chapter), fats are homely and recognisable.

What are fats chemically? The most common type of fat in the body is known as a triglyceride. The molecule is made up of a molecule of glycerol to which is attached three fatty acid molecules. The fatty acids themselves are composed of atoms of carbon and hydrogen closely linked together. When they are metabolised, used by the body's cell chemistry, the carbon becomes oxidised to carbon dioxide, the hydrogen joins with more oxygen to form water. So even on this outline you can see that a considerable amount of oxygen is needed when the cells 'burn' triglycerides. The result is that a great deal of heat energy is given out – as I have said, up to 300 calories from a single ounce.

In the past, people have spoken of 'fats' and left it at that, but triglycerids are beginning to appear in the literature. I expect we will hear more about them in the future and so, since they are the body's main form of energy reserve, and since they are a growing fashion, it is as well to have an outline understanding of what they are and how they work.

Triglycerides have one fatty acid bonded to the centre of the glycerol molecule and two more at each end, making a structure like a square capital letter Y. Other fats have just the single one at the centre (these are the monoglycerides); some others have only the one at each end (the diglycerides). Glycerol is better known as glycerine, incidentally, so that too is a familiar substance.

But are the fats saturated or unsaturated? And what do those terms mean? I have outlined the chemical structure of the glycerides in order to explain what the 'saturation' of fats involves. Everyone knows the terms, but fewer people know what they mean in practice. The distinction centres on those side-branches. In some fats, the hydrogen and carbon atoms are joined up in a form that means they are linked, as you might say, as closely as possible. Each atom has a set of side branches, with which the atoms can in effect bind to each other. Now, in a saturated fat, all the bonds of the side-branches are completely saturated. They are all joined up with each other.

In an unsaturated fat, some of the bonds are not fully saturated. That means they are more easily broken down. So they can be oxidised rather more easily than the saturated fats, and some unsaturated fats become rancid more rapidly than do the saturated fats. If there are a number of unsaturated bonds in the glyceride molecule, then the fat is said to be polyunsaturated.

In practice, saturated fats are typically solid, like lard. Unsaturated fats, by contrast, are typically runny (like oils). This outline of the principles of the two types is important, for it enables us to see that you can get some idea of the kind of fat you have from its properties. For example, it is now obvious that butter is probably rich in saturates, whilst soft margarine contains more polyunsaturates. We can now make unsaturated molecules into saturates in industrial processes which is why it is that palm oil can be hardened (i.e. saturated) to make soap, margarine or some other kind of fat. It also emphasises that the structure of fat depends on its molecular composition, and not just on where it originated. Hard margarine is rich in saturated fats, for instance, in spite of the popular belief that margarine is inherently 'safer' than butter. Margarine often contains animal fat, in spite of the belief that it comes from vegetable sources. Krona margarine is popularly

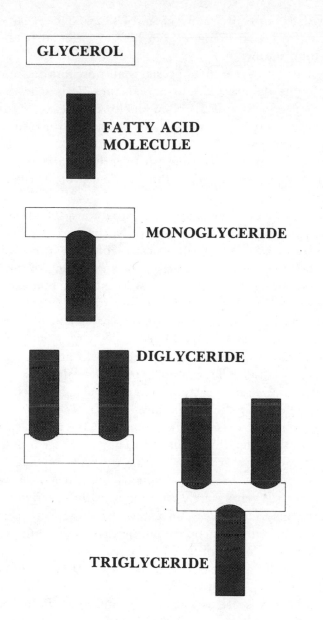

GLYCEROL

FATTY ACID
MOLECULE

MONOGLYCERIDE

DIGLYCERIDE

TRIGLYCERIDE

FAT MOLECULES. Fatty acids can join to a molecule of glycerol at three chemical sites, forming mon-, di-, and triglycerides. These are fats found in the body, as described in the text (triglycerides are set to become a fashionable buzz-word).

preferred to butter by many people I know since it is margarine, just that. In fact it is made from beef fat, and so is no better or worse than butter.

The current research suggests that polyunsaturated fats are better for us than are the saturated ones. It is true that the fat component of wild animals often has lower levels of saturated fats than does the fat from domesticated cattle and pigs, so it could be that our forbears ate less saturated fats than do we. It has also been shown that the oils from fish (clearly unsaturated fats) seem actually to protect against the incidence of heart attacks in humans.

This unexpected fact arose from studies of three different nationalities: Japanese, Spanish and Norwegian. At first sight it is not apparent what these countries might have in common. Look again and the anwer may emerge. It is that each of these nations has an exceedingly long coastline. A long coastline means a prominent and well-developed fishing industry. And so it has proved to be – the nations eating high proportions of fish also have a low incidence of coronary heart disease.

This is not because the people refrain from eating meat. The traditional eskimos, for example, remain healthy on a diet that never contained any vegetable matter – a fact which has posed many problems for the nutritionists who insist that we must have vegetables in our diets – and it seems to have been fish that gave the clue to their healthy ebullience. They often ate a pound of fish a day, which is more than we in the West would ordinarily consume. But they certainly ate plenty of meat too – it was not as though the fish were merely *replacing* meat in the diet.

That seems to be the case in a study from the Netherlands. Here it was shown that the people who ate extra fish actually ate more meat as well. They simply liked to eat meaty food, whether it derived from land or sea. The Dutch study showed that men who ate a few ounces of fish per week, or more, were half as likely to die from heart disease as a control population who never touched seafood. Most surprising of all was the fact that the men in the fish consuming group had higher levels of blood cholestorol. It seems the fish oils were in some way protecting against coronary disease and arterial disease, irrespective of the role played by the generally-recognised culprits.

The solution may lie in one specific polyunsaturated fat known

76

as EPA* which in the body seems to act against unwanted blood-clotting. Capsules of cod liver oil (rich in EPA) and similar preparations of a substance known, self-explanatorily perhaps, as Max-EPA, are used to treat patients with blood-clotting diseases and where there are clots in the coronary arteries. So why do I say only that EPA 'may' be involved? Simply because the Dutch research has also shown that two thirds of the patients in the study ate oily fish. The rest preferred to eat nothing but white fish, which contains virtually no EPA. Yet they were as well protected against coronary disease as were their oily fish-eating counterparts. So, though EPA does seem to have a recognisable action and play a part in treating blood vessel disease, it cannot be the whole answer.

Should we avoid saturated fats altogether? If you could magically remove all the saturated fats from your body you would die in convulsions. Remember that saturated fats are typically solid. This is because they perform important structural functions in the body. One of the best-known waxy, yellowish fats is cholesterol, which we know of for its unfortunate proclivity to turn up in plaques inside our blood vessels, where it produces blockages and causes heart attacks. Yet cholesterol is a vitally important part of our bodies. In the brain it makes up a significant proportion of the coating round the nerve cells and more particularly their branches. In the body it is involved in the manufacture of key hormones. In the gut it acts on food, aiding digestion, after it has been converted into bile salts in the gall-bladder. So cholesterol matters to us. In addition, it is produced in the liver in much larger amounts than we consume in our daily diet! We eat say 500 milligrams of cholesterol every day, yet two or three times as much is produced by the liver for the body's vital functions.

There is a clear argument in favour of cutting down cholesterol, if we are convinced that it crops up in diseased blood vessels and makes us ill. But we should not become fearful of the material, for it is vitally important to us. Even if we cut the amount of cholesterol in our diet to a minute proportion of what is normally eaten, it would make a much smaller impact on the levels of cholesterol in our bodies, because of the amount that the liver has to make. The orthodox view is this: Cholesterol occurs in damaged blood vessels; therefore eat less cholesterol. But we must understand that the

*Eicosapentoic acid.

picture is more complex. It is really something like this: cholesterol occurs in damaged blood vessels; it also occurs in important areas of our bodies where it plays a vital role; it is eaten in our daily food; it is made in much larger amounts by the liver; so cutting down excess cholesterol may be sensible, but is no immediate solution to our problems of artery disease. Even that is a crude summary of the complex story of cholesterol, but it is nearer the truth than the popular consensus.

For your ease of reference, here is a list of the higher-cholesterol foods.

1   FOODS CONTAINING MORE THAN 1000mg CHOLES-TEROL PER 100g. Brains, egg yolk.

2   FOODS CONTAINING MORE THAN 200 mg CHOLES-TEROL PER 100g. Caviar, fish roe, whole eggs, kidney, liver, butter, sweetbreads, seafoods (including crab, shrimp, lobster, oysters).

3   FOODS WITH 50–200 mg PER 100g.
Beef, lamb, pork, cheese, chicken, fish, ice-cream, veal, mixed margarine with animal fats.

4   SOME FOODS WITH ZERO CHOLESTEROL. Egg white, vegetable margarine, vegetables.

Am I suggesting that the body knows best? In many ways this is surely so. One popular view, to which I shall return when we look at dieting, is expressed thus: when excess energy-rich foods are taken into the body they are retained in the form of glycogen (an important short-term energy store). Once the glycogen levels are at their maximum, the excess protein, carbohydrate or fat is eventually synthesised into triglycerides and is laid down as a fatty deposit in the body. That is how people become overweight.

I am convinced this view is profoundly wrong. As it is a view which underpins the whole of our nutritional orthodoxy it is important I explain why I feel it is incorrect. The thesis depends on a belief of almost unimaginable stupidity, namely, that we evolved to limit our size by controlling the food we eat. People repeat this view in every textbook, yet ordinarily do not consider what this would entail in mathematical terms. At the risk of confusing unit systems (I do so to remain more easily understood by a non-metricated reader) let me illustrate what I mean.

Consider a man who consumes six grams more body-building food than he requires. That is an extra one-fifth of an ounce. In fat equivalent, that would be an extra 40 calories. This is such a tiny amount of additional food per day that in practical terms it would be unmeasurable. So here we have a man who eats *less than an extra 50 calories each day.* But this is 50 more than he requires, and so it is all stored and serves to make extra body mass. Eighty percent of the body is made up of water, and so the six grams dry weight of additional food would produce 30 grams (an ounce) of extra body tissues every day if it were being stored, as 'extra food' is said to be.

That seems like a pointlessly minute amount of additional food to consider, and indeed nobody could control their dietary intake with such exactitude. Yet, at the end of 70 years, that man would weigh over 1,500 lbs on top of his normal weight . . . He would have the mass of ten men, and all because he had eaten an extra six grams a day and put on seven ounces every week. Similarly, a person who consumed a slight amount less than he or she needed would fade away and vanish within a matter of weeks.

Nobody exists who is capable of such minute and accurate assessments of what they eat. No organism has evolved to take conscious actions by which to regulate its adult dimensions. Our size and weight are primarily controlled by our genetic consti-tution, and the limits at which our own 'internal switch' is set varies from person to person, and from age to age. There is clearly an *adipostat* – that is to say, a kind of 'thermostat' but which responds to how fat you are, rather than how hot. If an ounce of inaccuracy here and there could make one man weigh as much as ten, or another vanish in a few weeks, then nobody normal would ever exist. The astonishing thing about human beings in Western civilisations is not that one-third of them are overweight because we all eat too much. The key to that anomaly lies in the words by which it is expressed, for if we all eat too much we will all be overweight. It is a matter of observational fact that many individ-uals eat grotesquely huge meals and yet remain as slim as reeds, whilst others who are, if well-fed, certainly not greedy, end up obese, hot and sweaty.

It is not a simple question of metabolic rate, for the metabolic rate of fat people is usually higher than that of thin folk. There is extra body to undergo metabolism – and that is why our unhappy obese individual is hot and sweaty as well as fat. So the remarkable fact is not that one-third of us are overweight; it is the astonishing reality that *two-thirds of us are not*. What our bodies do is to assess how large or small we are supposed to be, and then any excess food we have consumed is harmlessly metabolised away and lost from the body through excretory mechanisms and respiration. Fat people are always being told by their doctors that they suffer from over-eating, and not from glandular abnormalities. That is misleading. They are fat because their adipostat is set differently from someone thinner's. It is not that they are merely 'greedy', for as I have shown an ounce here and there can add up to a huge difference, and in any event they often eat no more than their thin companions.

Fat people can lose weight by restricting their intake if they wish to, for you cannot lay down reserves if you are not eating any excess in the first place; but, just because you can lessen your weight by dieting, it does not follow that you were fat in the first place through gluttony. To pretend that was the case would be as logical as saying that a house catches fire through a lack of buckets, simply because you once used a bucket of water to put out a blaze somewhere else. Or that your leg was broken because of a lack of Plaster of Paris around it at the time. It is dangerous to invert logic like that. We are the size we are because that is what nature intended. We can cut down our size by restricting our food intake if that is what we wish to do, but this is a special case where mankind intervenes over destiny. For normal people, it is the body's own system of checks and balances that does the work.

The weight distribution often changes as people mature, and this too is probably because of contingencies with which our bodies have evolved. An episode of illness in an older person can produce wasting, and I guess that the tendency of people to become rather fatter as they pass through middle age is the body's way of arming itself against such contingencies.

Fats supply us with rather less than half of our energy supply, and carbohydrates supply a similar proportion. The remainder is made up by the burning of excess proteins for energy. Carbohydrates range from the simple (like glucose) to the complex (starches). A teaspoon of sugar gives an idea of a relatively simple carbohydrate, whilst a sample of cornflour will show what the starch end of the spectrum looks and feels like. Carbohydrates (like proteins) give up about four calories per gram, less than half as much energy as fats.

The simplest carbohydrates are the monosaccharides, including glucose. It is made up (as are all carbohydrates, and this is where they acquired their name) from atoms of carbon united with the molecules of water. In glucose you have six carbon atoms with six water-molecules (H_2O) making $C_6H_{12}O_6$. Next up in complexity are the disaccharides, each with twice as many carbon atoms. It is the disaccharide sucrose which is most familiar to us as sugar, its formula is $C_{12}H_{22}O_{11}$. From then we move on through a complex series of carbohydrates of increasing size (usually classified together as polysaccharides) up to the starches. As fats are an ultimate energy store in animals, starches along with oils are an ultimate energy store in the plant world. Since energy is primarily needed by the resting body of a plant, it is often in fruits (like the grains of corn) or tubers (like the potato) where the starch is laid down. Flour is what you obtain when you mill such a structure and release the stored starch.

There is an even more complex series of carbohydrates which humans cannot digest. These are such things as cellulose and lignin, of which plant fibres are composed. Fibre in the diet was considered a cranky subject for decades, but during the 1970s rose to become a highly fashionable and respectable topic of dietary conversation. Fibre as a substance is necessary for the gut to get to grips, so to speak, with the food it contains. Without fibre, the length of time it takes food to move through the intestinal tract from mouth to anus can become greatly increased, bringing with it the possibility of an increased risk of cancer-causing chemicals being formed; and they would have a similarly increased length of time to get into the cells. Without this form of movement the bowel can become distended and balloon-like pockets can form in the gut wall in a condition known as diverticulosis. In the USA it has been estimated that more than 15% of the population may suffer from this condition, and an increase in the levels of fibre in the diet is currently believed to be one answer to the problem.

Fibre even seems to act against the incidence of coronary heart disease. How is uncertain (some have argued that it absorbs extra cholesterol in the intestine, though this would not of course act against the larger amounts of cholesterol produced by the body.) There seems some good evidence for increasing the levels of fibre in the daily intake. A word of caution is that data do suggest that people who have a traditionally high-fibre diet also show raised levels of stomach cancer. It is impossible to demonstrate a cause-

and-effect relationship, but it does remind us that wholesale swings in dietary fashions do not always act in people's best interests.

Too much fibre can itself cause intestinal problems. A diet needs a sensible amount of this constituent – an excess can be just as bad as a deficiency, a fact the popular books overlook.

It is not necessary to eat bran as a source of dietary fibre, for any plant cell walls will do, and a few ounces of vegetables, fresh fruit, even peanuts (though beware of increasing your calorific intake, if you are trying out a reducing diet), can together provide raised levels of fibre without going to extremes.

Carbohydrates in the body are stored as glycogen, a kind of starch-like substance formed in the liver and elsewhere. Glycogen can be rapidly mobilised in the form of glucose, and it is as glucose that the body's cells like to obtain their supplies of energy for action. It is the burning of energy-rich substances which provides the motive energy for the reactions of life, and which also keeps us warm.

It is conventionally taught that the body is warmed by the 'waste' heat from the burning of carbohydrates in the muscles. This I feel is an inaccurate view: it may be more accurate to cite the liver as the main source of body heat, for it is here that the main chemical reactions go on which set in train the rest of the body's actions – the chemical balance of the blood is regulated by the liver, which acts as a kind of 'despatch centre' for the rest of the body. The blood comes out of the liver at a suitable tempera-ture, too, and it is better to see the liver as the organ which keeps us warm. Body metabolism does so too, but to think of that as the main source of the body heat may be erroneous.

Some people have realised that carbohydrates supply energy to the body – and often nothing else – and so have concluded that the elimination of carbohydrates from the diet would be the best way to slim. The argument is that, since proteins and fats can also supply energy but they are involved in building the body, then carbohydrates – which are purely used for energy – are not necessary and could sensibly be eliminated. That is not so. If carbohydrates fall much below 10% of the calories in the daily diet, the chemistry of fat metabolism is interrupted. Acetone appears on the breath, evaporating from the bloodstream in the lungs, and the blood becomes increasingly acid. In severe cases hallucinations occur and the patient may even collapse in a coma. In addition, such severe dieting can cause a loss of cells in the body, which

82

under those conditions tend to burn protein twice as fast as stored fats, to make up the deficit.

The amount of energy you need in a day – from whatever source – varies with your kind of lifestyle and also with your own body functions. Lying down motionless, you would burn about 1,500 calories in 24 hours*.

Asleep, as an example, you burn about 1 calorie per minute. Housework, driving, walking, rowing or dancing slowly would increase that to about 3 calories per minute. Cycling, canoeing, football and walking briskly would go above 5 calories per minute and such activities as climbing, cycle racing, hockey, jogging, skiing, squash or swimming would top 10 calories per minute. The swimming may surprise you momentarily until I explain that much of the heat loss here is to the surrounding water which (even in a warm pool) is always considerably cooler than the hot-blooded human swimmer.

A moderately active individual expends 2,500 calories a day. Yet how surprising it is that you would burn up more than half of that if you stayed in bed all day and did not so much as move a muscle. It is the continuous burning of energy in the body's cells that makes up that total. Clearly, much goes on.

*The figures are rather more for men, somewhat less for women. In this instance the normal range for women would be 1,200–1,500; for men 1,600–1,800.

CHAPTER SEVEN

I have outlined the essential building blocks from which living cells are constructed, the proteins, the fats and so on. And we have seen how the chemical reactions that we know as 'living' utilise the structural components of cells as a source of energy. Though proteins are the substance of which living cytoplasm is constructed, protein can also provide energy for life at the same rate as the burning by the cells of carbohydrate. In many ways I dislike using terms such as 'energy' and 'burning', let alone the 'chemistry of life', for all these notions ensnare us in the dogma of the body as a machine. The body is no such thing. The very fact that our living cells can utilise the same raw materials for such a range of purposes shows how life is a system, and not a structure; and the complex cybernetic network of regulation within living cells is something very different from an engineering notion of that term. Drive a machine 1,000 kilometres down the road and its tyres get thinner. Drive a human being down the road and the tyres get thicker. And if humans run short of fuel, why, they utilise the building materials from which they were made as a source of fuel. But you see – 'building materials': there we go again. In many ways we need a new vocabulary of words, and of ideas as well, with which to address this topic.

Here, too, I believe that the orthodoxies of science have been left behind by our need to understand ourselves and the real issues of living. Our terms are founded on a mechanistic view. Having discovered the principles of science, and elaborated a series of criteria by which we diagnose them, recognise what they do and then coin terms to communicate all this to other people, we now seek to fit these inappropriate terms and concepts onto living organisms for whom such trivial and obvious notions would be an absurdity. When I introduced the idea that a holistic view might be a sensible answer to the problems posed by treating cancer, for instance, in a leading article for a scientific journal, my words were picked up and I was gently teased for the coinage. That was in 1973, and it took a decade for opinions to reverse. The idea of holism is not scientific, for it becomes at once untestable, unrepeatable, individualistic and even subjective. You could look at acupuncture in a similar way, for that too is haunting, unprovable, unscientific, non-objective in many ways. It is for this reason that, at a time when we rate the scientific precept so highly, such notions are either unacceptable to the establishment, or at best find a grudging acceptance on (as the term has it) the fringe. On the one hand, you can clearly see why it is that the establishment should react against such ideas. It is too easy for people to pose as quacks if there is no scientific criterion by which to judge their ideas.

I have spoken to enough fringe medicos to know that they often do not know what they are doing, that they tend to blind people with esoteric terms to which the patient (the client, let us say) has no direct access; that they seem to seek more to impress the patient with a patronising and supportive aura of charismatic wisdom than really to get to grips with the realities of what is making them ill. Finally, they are usually more aware of the need to ensnare the patient in this strange and rigidly-observed ritual and to palm off the fruits of their specialism than they are devoted to clarity, approachability and openness. There is a kind of 'magicianship' about fringe medicine.

Much to my regret, the comments in the previous paragraph apply equally to the exponents of orthodox medicine. Substitute the words 'traditional doctor' for 'fringe medico' and the words ring as true. Though there are exceptions, it is a regrettable fact that many doctors retain just as much of a hold from mystique as do the worst fringe workers, and they are often quirky in the way they dispense cures. In British society we expect a doctor to be patronising, indeed it is almost a hallmark of any doctor that he has to be so. It is never a urinary infection, it is trouble with the old water-works; it is not a vaginal discharge, it is trouble up the old front passage.

85

As a student (I trust you will forgive me the irreverence) I was once asked by a nurse who came into my ward, 'Have your bowels moved this morning?' I folded down the top of the newspaper and said to her in tones as stentorian as you can manage at such a tender age, 'Moved? No, Nurse, they are in exactly the same place as last night. Though I did have an immensely satisfying crap at seven-thirty.' Yet if scientific research takes me into a hospital theatre these days I still wince when I hear staff ask respectable and venerable senior citizens – former diplomats, eminent romantic novelists, whatever – 'Wanna go to the lavvy for me?' with condescension.

The reason why we should recognise these deficiencies is that many of the alternatives do work. The view that a more holistic approach to cancer might be profitable now has some support from clinical results. And acupuncture seems to work, too. Orthodox medical spokesmen can afford to sneer at cranky recipes which do not seem to work, but not at novel concepts which really *do*. When you see a patient, plainly feeling no pain, yet fully conscious during surgery and treated only by the acupuncturist's needles, it is as plain as plain can ever be that it works. By that I mean that it works in a sense that can be objectively assessed, by any standards, as working. It satisfies the patient. It fulfils scientific criteria. Yet acupuncture is still seen to be essentially cranky and part of the fringe. Why? Only because it does not have a scientifically obvious explanation.

That may be an objection to the establishment, which is only hesitantly beginning to accept the procedure, but if we could accept that we are now past the era where science can always supply the answers, and where we need something new and less strictured, we would be able to marvel at the might of inexplicable processes which do give scientifically valid benefits. The placebo effect has already been recognised as challenging the efficacy of drugs under test, and is strenuously avoided because of the fact that it would interfere with the results – so surely medicine should recognise that it would be worth exploiting the effect, rather than always seeking to nullify it. The reason we do not is, as always, because it is not amenable to scientific examination. The nature of the process may not be scientifically assessable – but the results are. Our failure to understand why results from science having run its course. Truly, we do need something more up to date with which to work.

Meanwhile medical specialists, like fringe workers, like cranks, like charlatans, seek to exclude the outsider through the use of esoteric words and condescension. The confining of people to beds in hospitals is an instance of how the patient is subdued. Experts like to have you in nightwear, in bed, labelled as unwell and vulnerable. Why, you could not even walk outside like that. I have no doubt that if patients wore casual day clothes and met the medics more face-to-face then they would feel better quicker, and would be able to place medicine in a clearer perspective. Hospitals would be less like nurseries and more like comfortable and hospitable centres into the bargain.

It is not easy for a lay person to get to the truth of a complex issue like cancer and food. The proponents of the view that food causes cancer simply insist that processed foods cause cancer, so does refined sugar and every other refined food, and that is an end to the matter. The opponents of food argue that there is nothing dangerous about additives, so in they go and nobody should worry about them ever again. I would adopt a radically different approach. There is a need for us to set out our criteria for our beliefs. And I have to say that there is very little evidence to support the view that refined foods cause cancer to any significant degree. Indeed, refined foods are so pure that carcinogenic molecules creeping in would be less likely than for foods of less certain composition. There may be a psychological connection between indulgence and the fear of the body 'getting its own back', but there is nothing to show that cancer is caused by refinement. On the other hand, there are plenty of naturally-available foodstuffs that are rich in cancer-causing molecules. Cooking – if it produces a browning of food – increases the amount of carcinogenic chemicals present in the food.

It is also arguable that artificial additives are no worse in the cancer stakes than naturally available foodstuffs. But that would be no reason for their use if they could be avoided, since any increase in hazard is undesirable and, if we can keep the number of equally hazardous ingredients to a minimum (as is the case if you adopt the minimal interference principle), we keep potential risks to a minimum.

Above all, and a most important point to bear in mind no matter what your own viewpoint, there is a vast range of carcinogenic materials present in our ordinary diet. It is no good protesting that meat causes cancer, and so vegetarianism protects against it.

I have said that vegetarians suffer from cancer as do meat-eaters, and we will examine some of the potent agents that have so far been found in vegetable foods. Many vegetables are rich in carcinogens and mutagens*.

Before we consider some of them, just to see how varied they are, there is a point to bear in mind. The immediate conclusion you will already be drawing, doubtless, is that our food is a serious cause of cancer. It must be true that some cancers are caused by chemicals in food, but the simple relationship it is tempting to infer cannot be valid. I refer to something like this:

Carcinogens cause cancer;
Carcinogens are found in food we eat;
Therefore foods cause cancer.

This is too simple by far. If that were the case then everyone would contract cancer within a week or two and none of us would have survived to adulthood. In reality, carcinogens need to have specific circumstances in which to operate, they have to be brought into contact with the right cells, and possibly at the right time. Then the cell has to survive, and if it does it has to avoid being removed by the body's own protective mechanisms – which ordinarily mop up transformed cells efficiently – and at the end of the day the sequence has so many weak points that it is not a foregone conclusion that a cancer will result. Indeed the matter may not start. Carcinogens are liable to inactivation in the body, which has developed a range of protective mechanisms, and the chances of any given carcinogenic compound leading to a direct cause of cancer must be statistically tenuous.

I will outline some of the foods which are rich in carcinogens (and mutagens) and then look at the important anti-cancer mechanisms in humankind. You are then well armed to avoid foods that seem to you particularly risky (and there are one or two

*A carcinogen is a chemical that can transform a cell from its normal state into a malignant condition where it escapes from control and can form a cancerous growth. A mutagen is a substance which causes genetic mutations. In order to avoid loading this discussion with polysyllabic constructions more than necessary, I shall not endlessly repeat the two for they are often interchangeable. They occur when necessary for clarity in the discussion.

categories which I would warn against) and on the other hand you are equally well-placed to maximise your own protective mechanisms against cancers.

Many plant oils contain carcinogens and mutagens. Sassafras is rich in carcinogenic safrole, and is found in sarsaparilla (root beer) preparations. The related piperine turns up in black pepper and is known to cause cancer in mice. Cottonseed oil contains carcinogens, and the extract gossypol it contains is being tried as a male contraceptive in China, for even in small amounts it inhibits sperm formation. Some countries cook in cotton seed oil as a matter of course, and now plant breeders are trying to breed new strains which contain less gossypol. That seems a helpful measure, until you discover that the new strains are much more susceptible to infection by fungi such as *Aspergillus flavus*, and this produces aflatoxin which is itself a potent carcinogen.

This fungus is a frequent contaminant of foods that are poorly stored. It is common in peanuts, and many tests have shown that dried nuts and pulses can contain significant amounts of aflatoxin. The beans so fashionable these days are frequently bearers of carcinogenic compounds and mouldy foods in this category would be worth avoiding, so potent are they in aflatoxin. Fungi of the edible varieties often contain carcinogens, too. Some toadstools eaten by devotees contain high levels of hydrazines, many of which are known to be carcinogenic, and the common table mushroom has a small proportion of carcinogens.

The plants of the family *Umbelliferae* produce carcinogens and mutagens (these are plants that include carrots, celery, parsnips and parsley) and some data show that stressed or diseased celery can contain extremely high levels of these compounds – levels that are more than 100 times as high as the normal content. Celery is one of those plants that people always say you can eat in large amounts if you are on a diet. As I shall emphasise later on, I do not think any case can be made out for eating anything to excess on any kind of diet, and here is a case in point. I doubt whether celery or carrots ordinarily cause cancer – I certainly do not propose to curtail my own enjoyment of these delightful components of my own food intake – but instructing people, who do not know all the facts, to eat a substance which can sometimes contain a hundredfold increased levels of a known potent carcinogen is not necessarily sensible or helpful.

The nitrates have been raised as a possible health hazard in connection with their use in curing meat since they can form nitrosamines in the gut and these compounds are certainly potentially carcinogenic. But do not imagine that it is only the wilful excesses of humans who inflict such materials upon us: nitrates are also prominent in celery, lettuce, radishes, rhubarb and many root crops. A dose of about 200mg nitrate per 100g vegetable is typical. Tea and coffee are included in the category of vegetable extracts which contain carcinogenic compounds, for a cup of coffee containing about 100 mg caffeine also has more than twice that weight of the natural mutagen methylglycoxal. Caffeine itself may help potentiate the development of tumours initiated by other agents, and of course caffeine is present in teas as well as coffee – indeed it also occurs in drinking chocolate. A relative of caffeine, theobromine, which is characteristic of chocolate (though it also occurs in tea) is associated with damage to the DNA in cell nuclei. And there are other substances (including sterculic acid, quinones, quercetin and pyrrolizidine, to select a few) which are widespread through our diet and which are all known to be associated with damage to cells and with either mutations or cancer.

There is no comfort whatever for those who try to insist that raw vegetables are inherently 'safe' to eat. Nature has given us a rich and varied intake of dietary constituents, many of which on scientific evidence are extremely dangerous. A vegetarian diet is rich in carcinogens and mutagens, and meat as a rule is less likely to contain such compounds. There is a reason for the occurrence of poisonous and dangerous chemicals in vegetables, rather than in animals, since plant species often contain poisonous materials as a means of protecting themselves against predation or decay. Animal tissues which we eat rarely contain anything poisonous, for if they did they would also have poisoned the animal. There are traces of growth hormones and antibiotics, which result from the use of these substances in the rearing of animals under intensive conditions, and this is to be roundly deplored. Fortunately the banning of growth hormones is imminent, and controls on antibiotics should be much stricter than they were. It must be better to fit the farming orthodoxy to the animals, rather than the other way round; and that is a revolution in farming methods which is long overdue. The raising of animals under cramped and unsuitable conditions is cruel and inhumane, and the fact that we consume traces of substances like antibiotics, when we have no way of knowing they are there, is quite possibly dangerous as well.

90

But even if meat is naturally low in carcinogens, it acquires a significant proportion when it is charred. The cooking of meat, like the browning of any other food in the flame, leads to the production of carcinogens like benzpyrene. Grills and barbecues provide us with a source of this type of chemical. Rancid fats are a potent source of carcinogens. Since fat accounts for some 40% of the calories in a Westernised diet this could amount to a considerable load on the system.

But charred foods are not the greatest source of carcinogens that face us in our food. In the balanced daily diet we are faced with more carcinogens from natural sources than we are from man-made interference. The American Chemical Society's publication *Chemical Carcinogens* shows that the levels of benzpyrene and benzanthracene produced in a barbecued steak can be greatly exceeded by the levels found in naturally grown vegetables. Part of these data are as follows:

Foodstuffs	Benzpyrene	Benzanthracene
	(Expressed In Parts Per 100,000)	
Coconut oil	44	98
Fresh Vegetables	3–25	0.3–44
Cooked sausage	13–19	18–26
Barbecued ribs	11	4
Charcoal-broiled steak	8	5
Smoked ham	3	3

Benzpyrene (more accurately benzo (a) pyrene, but let us stay with the traditional shorthand version) and benzanthracene are both polycyclic aromatic hydrocarbons. Thirteen of these have been found in food so far, but less than half are carcinogenic. Even here we have to be careful in looking at the scientific findings. A paper published in 1967 showed that rats fed a diet containing up to 40 micrograms of benzpyrene per day developed no tumours, but those in which the administration was doubled to 80μg per day developed tumours of the squamous region of the stomach. This result has often been quoted.

But there are two additional points. The first is that we have no such region in our stomachs; ours are all glandular and not squamous (a squamous region of the stomach is a region that is smooth, like the inside of your cheek, and though it is found in many animals – like the rat – it is absent from human stomachs). The rats showed no tumours whatever of the glandular portion, which suggested that this region is more resistant to carcinogenic influences. The second point is to emphasise that there is a detoxifying complex formed by the glands of the intestinal tract which can act against polycyclic hydrocarbons (the aryl hydrocarbon hydroxylase system) and this serves to protect us against many of these theoretically damaging influences.

So do not panic unecessarily about charcoal-barbecued foodstuffs. Firstly, they contain less carcinogenic material than many fresh vegetables; secondly, they do not show a high likelihood of damaging the human intestine, compared with some other experimental models; thirdly we have ways of handling them which further reduce the risk they pose. It may seem like common sense to refrain from eating foods in which the levels of polycyclic hydrocarbons have been knowingly increased, or to refrain from eating them incessantly; but it is equally important not to burden ouselves with a spurious fear that we are on the point of suffering dreadful consequences through eating dinner. That form of stress certainly can result in ill-health.

The evidence against artificially synthesised, new food additives is not always easy to interpret. In some cases experiments have been poorly designed or inefficiently interpreted. Two food colours, Ponceau 3R and Ponceau MX, were both withdrawn from use following research in the 1960s which showed them to be carcinogenic. A further colour, Brilliant Blue FCF (E133), was later tested on mice which developed kidney tumours. But mice normally develop kidney tumours. It was later suggested that the incidence seen was within the limits that mice might normally suffer, without consuming any suspect additive.

The emotional interpretation of research is always a danger in this controversial area. For instance, the banning of cyclamates as sweeteners followed research in the late 1960s which associated cyclamates with bladder cancer in rats. The 'Delaney Clause' in the USA calls for the immediate ban on any substance associated with causing cancer, and so cyclamates were banned. They are also banned in the UK, though they are on sale elsewhere as sweeteners and I always try to obtain some when I am in a country where they are available. Why? Because cyclamates are an excellent means of sweetening drinks. They have a pleasantly sugary taste and lack the bitter aftertaste of saccharin. The cancer risk is very likely non-existent. What was widely overlooked when cyclamates were under scrutiny was that when they were first tested on their own they produced no evidence of carcinogenicity. It was when they were tested in combination with saccharin that suspicions arose. It was the cyclamate that was banned, not the saccharin, but the evidence against cyclamates was very slight and in scientific terms there must be a million items of the daily diet against which there could be more evidence.

In some cases carcinogens may even be made in our bodies. There is believed to be an association between the eating of fatty substances and the incidence of cancer of the colon. It may be that the fats are metabolised by organisms that live in the intestine, and they then produce carcinogens which affect the lining of the colon. A reduction in high levels of fat in the diet would be sensible for several reasons, and this is an added justification.

Furthermore, it has been shown in several experiments that the simple act of cutting down the calorific value of the daily diet in animals can reduce their likelihood of developing cancers. It is generally accepted that we all eat too much in the West, and if that is so then a reduction of calorie intake would not only help your waistline, but could be a first-line defence against cancer and the factors which encourage cancers to develop.

Let us look at how the body is protected against these factors. One of the main anti-cancer agencies in the body is the mopping up of transformed cells by the immune response. Often a cancer forms, not just because of carcinogenesis, but rather because the body's immune system is temporarily unable to recognise the 'rebel' cell and thus eliminate it. A tumour may be the result of the body's inability to eliminate the growth, rather than of any new assault by a carcinogen.

The body's surfaces are always being renewed. The skin, the lining of the intestinal tract, the stomach and oesophagus are in a state of continuous renewal from beneath. New cells grow up from the germinal layer at the base of the skin and those on the top are shed. In this way cells that may have been exposed to carcinogens are regularly replaced. The body itself detoxifies carcinogens by processing within the cells whenever that is possible, and in any event the healthy intestine passes food and its residues at a rate

93

that is usually too rapid for carcinogens to act. This is one of the benefits of a diet adequately supplied with bran and roughage, for the transit times are kept to a minimum when the gut can handle bulky food successfully. The moist and pap-like food, largely devoid of roughage, which some people try to eat causes the gut contents to lie around for longer than normal, and in that case there is a greater chance for carcinogenic materials (like nitrosamine) to form in the intestine, and a longer time for it to act.

So obviously there are some measures you might take if you were anxious about cancer. The first thing is to recognise that it would be impossible to eat a diet that was completely free of any carcinogenic or mutagenic compounds. No such diet exists. Stories about people in mountainous areas or distant jungle tribesmen who eat a cancer-free diet are nonsense. They may rarely suffer from cancer, but they are certainly eating plenty of carcinogens and mutagens in their daily food. So you cannot avoid them. What is more, your body knows that, and is already well able to take care of much of the burden without any intervention from outside. Just remember that carcinogens are natural, and that the mechanisms for dealing with them have evolved over millions of years. In most cases, the challenge of a carcinogenic molecule is well controlled by the body.

The second thing to do is to try to avoid eating excessive amounts of foods that are rich in carcinogens. Do not eat bad or mouldy vegetables and pulses. In this way you are controlling the intake of aflatoxins from pulses that have a slight fungus contamination, and you should automatically reject diseased celery or carrots. Enjoy a barbecued steak by all means – what would summer be like without the aroma of a barbecue in the background? But do not eat masses of barbecued food, and do not eat it all the time. Avoid rancid fat or stale cooking oils. Note that there is no need to write a list of dos and don'ts: what I am saying is that it may be a bad thing to eat mouldy and stale vegetables, rancid fats and endless barbecued steaks. Our senses already suggest that these would be natural things to avoid – the term 'rancid' connotes unpleasantness – so this is not a course of action that people would find revolutionary. Following your natural instincts would be a close approximation to what I am suggesting.

Next, pay attention to the items in your diet that will potentiate the anti-cancer functions in your body. One of the easiest is to ensure a bulky diet. I do not altogether go along with the view that you should eat so much bran that your faeces float in the pan; faeces as a rule sink in water, no matter what species they come from, and it is probably as well they do. My view of floating faeces is that they contain gas produced by organisms that are trying to break down the bran and its components. No, the diet need not contain bran, but should essentially contain plant matter – apples, fresh vegetables, nuts, anything like that – which will keep the gut contents active and healthy, and will keep transit times – from mouth to anus – down to a normal limit. In this way the food passes through at a healthy rate and does not hang around as though looking for damage to cause.

Uric acid acts against carcinogenesis and occurs in the saliva, so it may be that it is a first line of defence against carcinogens in the diet. But high levels of uric acid produce gout, and so it should not be increased in the hope of cancer prevention. Ascorbic acid in the diet, vitamin C, is a strong antioxidant and helps to inactivate carcinogenisis. There is an argument that very large doses could produce problems of their own, but a few hundred grams per day in the diet would probably be reassuring. Vitamin E, tocopherol, is believed to protect against genetic damage, and so adequate levels of this vitamin would be helpful too. It is not known what are the symptoms of vitamin E deficiency, since people without enough in their diet are never observed, but raised levels would probably work against the cancer risk and so could be added to your list. The carotenes which are abundant in coloured vegetables have been shown to be anti-cancer agents in animals, and likely to have the same effect in humans. Here, too, adequate supplies in the diet would help keep the mind at peace. Of the minerals, it is likely that selenium is an anti-cancer element. It has been shown to protect against the induction of tumours in experimental animals, and some authorities claim that low levels of selenium in the diet are associated with cancer in humans.

Sources of these substances in the diet are listed below:

Sources of Roughage
Vegetables and fruits, pulses and nuts.

Sources of Vitamin C
Citrus fruits, green peppers and parsley, effervescent tablets containing up to a gram of ascorbic acid. But do not overdose with these: people who take several tablets per day run the risk of

causing a condition, like gout, in which crystals form in the joints with painful consequences.

Sources of Vitamin E
Seed oils, including soy bean, corn and safflower. Also present in margarine. Most concentrated source of cotton seed oil, which is unfortunately also a potent source of gossypol.

Carotenes
Green and yellow fruits and vegetables, including carrots, sweet peppers, apricots, spinach. Red palm oil is very high indeed in carotenes.

These are measures one can personally take to minimise the risks from too many carcinogens in the diet, and to maximise the body's protection against these carcinogens when they do occur. Above all, it must be understood that a carcinogen does not simplistically 'cause' a cancer as a match causes a fire. Nature has weighted the chances very firmly against the carcinogen, and the body has elaborate and subtle ways of minimising damage. To me it seems prudent to know where the highest exposures come from, and how to avoid them; but even this may be unnecessary for we have no proof that these agencies actually produce a cancerous cell in a human body. What I suggest is that we cannot ask for a scientific answer, for there are too many variables. What we can do instead is to weigh up the available evidence in a fashion that satisfies our own criteria. On that basis there is little to fear from our normal daily diet – but steering away from the most potent sources of possible hazard does seem to be prudent.

CHAPTER EIGHT

It was discovered in 1912 that a diet which was rich enough in proteins and fats, minerals and carbohydrates, was not sufficient for animals to thrive. They needed something else. The missing components seemed to be one of the chemical group known as amines, and as they seemed to be vital for survival, and concerned with vitality, they were named *vitalamines*. Since that time the Gallic 'e' has gone, and we know more of the chemical structure (they were not necessarily amines at all), but the name is basically with us to this day. Now the production of vitamin pills and potions is big business. There are even some new potions in the shops which are described as vitamins, but are actually nothing of the sort.

Vitamins are complicated structures in chemical terms, though in almost every case we can now manufacture them in the laboratory. They are required in very small amounts, but are none the less vital for the proper conduct of the chemistry of living. Over-dosage is a problem for many of them, and for the average diet there is enough intake of vitamins to keep entirely healthy. But first I should introduce them individually so that we can establish the ground rules for the further study of what a vitamin is, and what it can do to us.

Vitamin A

RETINOL

This is a pale yellow fatty solid which dissolves in oils but hardly at all in water. It is found in milk and dairy produce, margarine and fish oils. Another good way of obtaining vitamin A is through green plants which contain carotenes. These can be synthesised in the body into vitamin A even though the vegetable itself contains none of the actual vitamin. So vegetables are a good source of what used to be called pro-vitamin A, and should be a part of any balanced diet. The best source of the vitamin in concentrated form is liver.

Vitamin A was not the first to be identified, for it was not until 1930 that it was discovered and named at the University of Wisconsin. The vitamin is most widely known for its involvement in eyesight. It is said that there were many cases of blindness in Danish children during the First World War, when the government skimmed all the domestic milk production in order to make butter which was sold abroad to pay for armaments. The Danish children were deprived of their vitamin A in the process, and cases of blindness resulted. There are hundreds of thousands of cases of blindness in India at the present time, due to the lack of vitamin A in the dietary intake.

This vitamin is needed for healthy metabolism, for normal development and growth and for healthy skin, quite apart from its importance in vision. A lack of the vitamin causes night blindness, a fact discovered at the beginning of this century by fishermen from Canada and Scotland, who found that liver in the diet prevented them from developing night blindness.

It is important not to take too much, for vitamin A is known to kill in excessive amounts. There have been cases of addicts to carrot juice and vitamin A pills who died of the overdosage, and of children who died whilst being overdosed by zealous but misguided mothers. There are high levels of the vitamin in polar bear liver, for example, and the eskimo folk-lore prohibits the eating of this organ for it is so rich in vitamin A that it proves rapidly fatal. The vitamin can be stored in the body, so a portion of liver once a week would provide quite enough vitamin A for health. It is recommended that about 5,000 International Units per day are taken in the diet; but ten or twenty times as much are acceptable. Overdosing, though, is distinctly dangerous.

Vitamin B group

THIAMIN

Thiamin was known as vitamin B_1, and was the first vitamin to be discovered. The research was carried out by Dr Casimir Funk in 1911 and it was this Polish scientist who originally named his discovery vitalamine. He was not the first to notice the effect of the vitamin deficiency. That had been recorded more than 3,000 years ago. Lack of thiamin effects the nerves, causing difficulty in moving and paralysis. The disease that results has long been known as beri-beri. Thiamin is present in the husks of rice, but is absent from white rice when the husks have been removed. For this reason it was gradually recognised that white rice was associated with beri-beri, and this became widely accepted in the 1880s. At that time the new 'germ theory of disease' was the latest innovation on the medical front, and so the research workers did not search for a chemical component missing from the rice: rather, and with some justification at the time, they decided that there was a bacterium in the white rice which was causing the disease. It was Funk's separation of the pure vitamin from the hulls of rice that eventually proved that beri-beri was due to a *lack* of a vital component in the diet, rather than the *presence* of a disease germ. The body needs about ½ milligram per day of thiamin for the tissues to be saturated with it. Most people consume about twice or three times as much, and there is no evidence that overdosage can cause problems. The main sources of thiamin in our diet are meat, vegetables and yeast (yeast is the richest source of all). Pork, bacon, kidney, bread and pulses are all high in thiamin.

RIBOFLAVIN

Originally known as vitamin B_2, riboflavin is found in the same places as thiamin, notably in liver, meat, milk and green vegetables. The daily requirement is rather more than that of thiamin, and again there is no knowledge of overdosage. A lack of the vitamin produces premature ageing, skin and eye disorders and anaemia. However, once again it is important to emphasise that, at a dose of slightly more than 1½ mg per day, the body's cells are effectively saturated with as much riboflavin as they need. So, though a shortage may cause premature ageing, an overdosage will not in some magical way slow the ageing process. The vitamin is stored for short periods, so a regular supply from a varied diet is essential. In most diets there is plenty of riboflavin.

NIACIN (NICOTINIC ACID)

This B vitamin was first known as a product of the analysis of nicotine – which is where the name 'nicotinic acid' came from! However it is not obtained from smoking and when in 1937 it was recognised as a vitamin of general importance it was renamed niacin in order to escape the associations with a somewhat unhealthy substance. A third name is niacinamide, but this is rarely used and is confined in normal practice to the United States.

A lack of niacin causes pellagra, a word meaning *rough skin*. The disease is still widespread in parts of the tropics, though it was first described in the eighteenth century and was recognised during the US Civil War. A lack of niacin can cause symptoms known for short as the 3 D's: dermatitis, dementia and diarrhoea. 15–20 mg of niacin per day are the normal requirement and a mixed diet produces plenty of supply under normal circumstances. There is a good deal in meat and fish – including canned fish such as sardines and salmon – and niacin is added to flour and used in bread-making. About a quarter of our daily intake is from flour and baked goods made with fortified flour containing the synthesised vitamin.

Niacin is known to cause headache, liver damage and nausea in high doses in excess of, say, 300 mg per day. Only the over-zealous use of vitamin pills would lead to this degree of excess.

Vitamin B_{15} PANGAMATE

This is, or perhaps 'was' would be more accurate, a substance claimed to act as a miraculous vitamin. Bottles sold under this name prove to have contained a range of substances, including a complex mutagenic compound at one end of the scale, right down to the less exotic milk-sugar, lactose, at the other. Pangamate, or 'vitamin B_{15}', was actually patented in 1949 in the United States. However it is not necessary for a patented invention under US law to work, to be what it says it is, or to do what it is claimed to do. Pangamate was said to be an extract of fruit stones which would treat a host of conditions. Within a few years several other workers had repeated the findings and the product became better known. Eventually it seemed that the substance had been illusory, and its benefits imagined. There is no 'vitamin B_{15}' and the matter remains an intriguing sidelight on the ease with which belief in science can be led astray.

PYRIDOXINE
(Pyridoxol, pyridoxal, pyridoxamine) = Vitamin B6
This vitamin is widespread and is associated with the B vitamins already discussed. Once more, a deficiency of this vitamin on its own is rarely found in populations fed a good mixed diet. The

main sources are offal, meat and wheat germ. There is some evidence from studies on babies fed on artificial diets, rather than breast-milk, that a deficiency of pyridoxine can cause nervous disorders. It is also possible that more than the normal 2 mg per day are required by women taking oral contraceptives. Anaemia, weight loss and depression are associated with a lack of pyridoxine in women taking the pill, though of course this could be a parallel effect and due to other causes. No danger of overdosage exists. Some unsuccessful experiments were carried out on schizophrenic patients who were given 4,000 times the normal daily dose, but, though no reliable improvement in the schizophrenia was seen, there was no evidence of vitamin toxicity either.

PANTOTHENIC ACID

The name means 'coming from everywhere' and this is another of the B vitamins which occurs widely associated with the others. No natural evidence of deficiency has been seen, but experiments with animals have shown that a range of disorders set in resulting in death. Gross overdosage can kill too, though only in amounts that are thousands of times greater than the normal daily requirement of around 5–20 mg per day. Pantothenic acid is involved with a range of metabolic systems and is vital for the formation of hormones in the body. The main sources of the vitamin are meats, cereals, pulses and nuts.

BIOTIN

Though meat and offal are good sources of this B vitamin, it is also found in milk and bananas. In life it is bound to proteins, and indeed it will bind to raw egg white in the intestine and in this way avoid absorption by the body. This was first noted in rats who were fed a diet of uncooked egg white as their source of protein. They became unwell and died, and it transpired that what was happening was that the biotin in the diet was being bound to the egg white and was thus inactivated. Later, some human cases were noted in which raw egg white was consumed in a diet that was already low in biotin. Skin changes occurred, anaemia appeared and the patients became weak and over-tired. Here too it was the egg white which was interfering with the absorption of the biotin in the food. Cooked egg white does not have the same effect.

In normal circumstances deficiency is not seen. The amount required in the diet is estimated to be around 100–300 microgrammes per day. Far more than this is passed out in the faeces, however. Doubtless this is because bacteria in the intestinal tract themselves manufacture the vitamin and we do not absorb all that they release.

CHOLINE
This widespread vitamin is readily available in the diet and the only cases of deficiency we have studied are those that have been experimentally produced in rats. In these experiments fatty liver and kidney disease appears. Choline can be synthesised in the body's own cells and so it is not a strictly essential vitamin component in the diet.

COBALAMIN (Vitamin B_{12})
A lack of vitamin B_{12} – as it is still widely known – produces a severe and slowly progressive anaemia. Some people, even though they eat enough B_{12} in the diet, lack a substance known as intrinsic factor which separates the B_{12} from the food in which it is found, and enables it to be absorbed by the body. Those who lack this factor suffer from a genetic inability to utilise B_{12}, and this results in the formerly much feared disease – pernicious anaemia. B_{12} is vital for the successful formation of the haemoglobin we need to carry oxygen around the body. Without it the patient is doomed to a slow and lingering illness.

The dose of B_{12} needed every day is exceedingly small, effectively less than a millionth of a gram. B_{12} is only found in animal food-stuffs and is absent from all vegetables. But a person who suddenly gave up all animal foods would not develop any symptoms for five years or so, because the amounts stored in the liver would be enough to supply the needs of the haemoglobin-manufacturing process for that length of time, so tiny is the daily amount consumed.

The recommended dose every day is stated to be higher than the amount consumed, to allow for failure of absorption. The formula for the vitamin, which was first found in 1948 and is a red crystalline compound, is unnusually complex for a vitamin:

$$C_{63}H_{90}O_{14}N_{14}PCo$$

For this reason of molecular complexity it has not been synthesised in the laboratory, and is the only vitamin to remain beyond the reach of the industrial chemist. It was traditionally extracted from liver though it took one tonne of the liver to produce a single gram of the vitamin. More recently it has been produced from microbes grown in biotechnology plants, and so it is now available from industrial sources; but synthesis continues to elude us.

The vitamin is widespread in animal foods and a normally mixed diet will easily provide more than the requirement. Overdosage has not been reported.

FOLIC ACID

This vitamin was first isolated in 1946 and it is now known to be a term that covers several related substances. It is similar in its function to B_{12}, and is vital for the formation of new DNA. It is required in small amounts, typically about 100 micrograms per day, and a normal diet exceeds this by a wide margin. It is a widespread vitamin, being found in liver, kidney, egg yolk (also a good source of B_{12}) and green vegetables (notably spinach). Vulnerable groups of people, notably the elderly and the pregnant, may be liable to a deficiency which causes anaemia, amongst other things. It is said that taking excessive folic acid can mask an underlying lack of B_{12} by providing a false negative result in the biochemical tests used to detect pernicious anaemia. In those cases there would be a risk of neurological disease, though cases like that are rare.

Vitamin C

ASCORBIC ACID

A glass of fresh orange juice every morning provides the basic requirement for vitamin C, a substance that is not stored by the body and is readily destroyed by cooking.

Put like that it seems simple, yet scurvy dogged the heels of travellers for thousands of years and led to countless deaths. The failure of the Scott expedition to the South Pole in 1912 was due to the fact that no fresh fruit and vegetables were available to provide them with vitamin C, and they became ill with scurvy.

Vitamin C has many effects in the body, one of them being its action as an anti-oxidant in protecting against cancer (discussed on p 95). But it is, most importantly, a component of the manufacture of collagen, the connective substance which structurally holds cells together. Without vitamin C, collagen fails. Patients develop sores, the heart muscle develops lesions as it actually starts to come apart, and old wounds – which healed when bands of collagen united the scarred and damaged edges – open up again.

Many explorers who wrote about the outbreaks of scurvy amongst their men described how long-forgotten wounds reappeared and gaped open exactly as they had done on the day they were inflicted – even though they had healed perfectly and had been closed ever since.

The early work on the scourge of scurvy is a classical example of the way in which an unfashionable view will not be accepted by the establishment no matter how sound the evidence surrounding it. Matters in that respect have not altered very much.

The key work on scurvy was done by James Lind, a Scottish surgeon, who published his observations in 1753. He had carried out some experiments in which he gave groups of sailors different diets, trying in each case to test one or other of the old-wives'-tales about how scurvy should best be treated. He fed different groups diets including vinegar, garlic, salt, alcohol . . . and one group were fed on a diet that included two oranges per day. The results were unquestionable. The sailors who ate the oranges did not develop scurvy. It was a clear-cut result, which Lind hastened to present to the Royal Society of Medicine in London.

It would be comforting to assume that the medical world stood back in admiration and commended him for his humanitarian diligence. In fact (and this will come as no surprise to those who have followed what I have said earlier about bias, fashionism, and irrationality) they laughed him to scorn.

It was entirely unacceptable to the establishment at that time, that a disease could be prevented by a simple change of diet. Nowadays the polarisation runs counter to this: we imagine that a change of diet can explain almost any state of mankind, and it is close to heretical to suggest anything else. Lind continued to campaign from time to time, but he was an active research worker and did not brood on the single topic that he had so successfully resolved. He did other research too, showing for example that the water distilled from sea-water was drinkable, and working out a system of obtaining potable water for ships long at sea. He died in 1794. The following year the Royal Navy recommended that lemon juice should be issued to sailors, and scurvy was banished in a short while. It was over a century before Lind's findings were adopted internationally. But his work was clear-cut and decisive and is an excellent example of how to tackle a research project – and an equally revealing example of the way that establishment can react.

The possibility that vitamin C acts against the common cold has often been raised in the past and, some claim, conclusively proved. I have yet to see any data that show vitamin C prevents colds, or even makes them milder once they have been contracted. However, I should declare my own standpoint, which is exemplified by an answer I gave to a questioner in Singapore. He asked whether there was any evidence to suggest that vitamin C worked against the cold virus. As my lecture had been on a different subject altogether I did not have a prepared or considered judgment to offer, and what I said was this: 'I have looked closely at the evidence over vitamin C and the common cold many times in the past, and I may honestly say that I have seen no definitive evidence that shows the vitamin either prevents or lessens the severity of a virus infection. However, whenever I think I am getting a cold or a bout of 'flu, I take half a gram of vitamin C every day and I have not suffered from a bad cold for several years.'

As I said to the questioner, I hope that throws some light on the matter.

Vitamin C can be taken in larger doses, say around half a gram or a gram a day, in the hope that it acts as a protective against disease. More than that would be entirely without value, and indeed higher dosages could result in the formation of crystals in the joints which in turn could cause a disease like gout. So, excessive overdosing is inadvisable.

Vitamin D

CALCIFEROL

Vitamin D is produced in the body by the action of sunlight on the skin. The deficiency first appeared in European society when people began to move from the countryside into the newly expanding industrial towns during the 1600s. They were, for the first time, spending their time indoors and the smoggy and smoky atmosphere greatly reduced the amount of sunlight they received. So, much less vitamin D was made in their skin, and rickets began to appear.

The symptoms of rickets result from the bowing of the legs that occurs when the calcification of the long-bones is not satisfactory. It is a condition that is still sometimes seen in immigrant communities in white nations, which raise children in conditions of far less sunlight than they were used to at home.

105

Vitamin D abounds in fish oils, notably halibut liver oil. It occurs almost exclusively in animal-originated foods, but synthetic vitamin D is added to margarine as a dietary supplement. There is only a trace in cheese and milk. It is 7-dehydrocholesterol in the skin (a relative of cholesterol) which is the source of the vitamin D liberated by the action of sunlight, and any other source of ultra-violet light will suffice. Thus, a sun-ray lamp would prevent rickets in children whose diet was deficient in the vitamin. In adults it is believed that most of the vitamin D used in the body is produced in the skin through sunlight, so dietary minima are hard to establish.

For at-risk groups, vitamin D supplements are available. But overdosage is a danger. The amount that is needed to sustain a healthy existence without any sunlight exposure is set around 300 International Units, but at 1,000 I.U. – a scant three times as much – the kidneys may become calcified and cease to function, whilst at double that level (2,000 IU) fever, irritability, vomiting and diarrhoea set in. Overdose of vitamin D can prove fatal. However it is often recommended that sensible supplements in the form of fish liver oil capsules should be taken by growing children.

Vitamin E

TOCOPHEROL

Vitamin E has long been dubbed 'the sex vitamin' since rats fed on a diet absolutely lacking this substance become infertile. However it is not known what effect it has on adults and no examples of deficiency are known. Vitamin E seems to exert a significant action against the transformation of normal cells into cancerous ones, and it seems to exert a generally protective effect against cells being damaged by the oxidation of unsaturated fats. It is also concerned with haemoglobin synthesis. The major sources of vitamin E have been discussed on p 96, but supplements are available for those who wish to have them in tablet form. There is little evidence that they have a significant effect, and claims of an almost mystical nature that vitamin E acts in treating heart disease and burns, quite apart from boosting sexual prowess, have little evidence to support them. But, chemically, tocopherol is an antioxidant and so could protect against cancer; it has few signs of being dangerous in excess (there are reports that it caused blurred vision and fatigue in one group who took too much) and it may yet have secrets to reveal.

Vitamin K

This is a substance closely involved in the blood-clotting process. It is produced by bacteria that inhabit the intestinal tract and it is then absorbed by the body. No overdosage has been reported, and the amount taken in by the dietary route seems to be insignificant compared with the amount of vitamin K produced by our resident microbes. The nearest we come to observing a deficiency is when massive doses of antibiotics are administered, which wipe out the gut flora and leave the patient without his or her resident organisms.

The formula for vitamin K is known to be $C_{21}H_{46}O_2$ but there is a simpler molecule known as 'vitamin K analogue' which is easier to produce in the laboratory and which has the same effects, but which is approximately twice as powerful. This is used in cases where there is a deficiency in the blood-clotting process.

Minerals and Trace Elements

The main mineral in the human body is calcium, followed closely by phosphorus. It is a form of calcium phosphate which makes up bones. The main chemical constituent of the body fluids is salt, sodium chloride, which is why they all (tears, urine, perspiration, etc.) taste salty. In the dissolved form in which salt occurs in the tissues, it is separated into the two components of which it is made – that is to say, the sodium and the chloride act in their own specific way. So in general terms it is better to speak of how much chloride there is, for example; it might have come into the body in the form of calcium chloride or potassium chloride, but once it is dissolved in the tissues it is just the chloride ion no matter where it came from. What is very important from the viewpoint of the cells from which we are made is the *ratio* between the different elements. Thus the sodium:potassium ratio is carefully regulated in the body and if it becomes upset through some major shock to the system then symptoms – like nervousness – can appear. However in the normal way we consume more than enough of each, and the body works the rest out for itself.

Sodium

Living tissues need sodium and we take in plenty with our food. In the tissues, sodium remains largely outside the cells, and is

107

found in the fluid that bathes them. Cells originally became developed in sea-water, and the body keeps its own cells living in a sea-water-like environment to this day. We add sodium to our diet as salt, and there is some relationship between the amount of salt taken in each day and the development of high blood pressure in those who are susceptible to it. It seems as if those with a predisposition to heart trouble are the ones who are at risk, for there is no evidence that everyone taking too much salt is at a greater risk from hypertension. However, in some cases you may not find out which category you are in until too late; so there is some sense in keeping salt in the diet down to a low level, since there is already much present in food from natural sources. But you do not have to limit the amount until it exactly balances what your body needs to retain, for urine is always salty (except in abnormal states of health) and excess salt is excreted. Some folk do tend to imagine that you have to monitor carefully the intake so that it is within strict limits, rather as some people construe the need to monitor your intake of food. But the body has evolved to extract what it needs and to pass out the surplus as waste, and all living things have done this since life itself began, so there is no need to assume that humans, suddenly, have to take over this complex task by conscious effort. There are altogether 80 grams of sodium in the average body, 2–3 ounces.

Potassium
Potassium is, like sodium, obtained from many dietary sources. As sodium bathes the cells, potassium is found mainly within them. The body takes in 2–5 grams of potassium a day, roughly the same as the amount of sodium, and the total in the body is 130 grams. Potassium chloride is sometimes used to replace part of the sodium chloride (salt) in foodstuffs, and that is a perfectly healthy thing to do. Fruit juices are typically high in potassium so there is some good sense in a glass of juice with breakfast.

Calcium
Sodium is perhaps the most fundamentally important metallic ion found in the body, but calcium is the most abundant. There is 1 – 1½ kg calcium in the average human adult, about 3 lb, most of it in combined form in the bones. But calcium in the dissolved form is vitally important in many of the body's reactions – in blood-clotting, the function of the nerves and muscles – and is part of the cell structure, involved both in balancing the ratio of acid

to alkali, and in the formation of the materials which cement the cells together. Though calcium is vital for cells, it is not very soluble in water and many organisms have a solid body tucked away somewhere which acts as a calcium reservoir. Some excess calcium is laid down in this contingency reserve, and is liberated into the cell fluids when amounts run low. Bear this mechanism in mind, I think it will help to make sense of where bones originated. They were originally calcium reservoirs, which as the body of animals became more specialised were adapted into their role as attachment points for muscles and for supporting a body structure. The relevance of the 'calcium reservoir' theory is that, in people with low levels of calcium in the diet, the mineral will be released from the bones in order to maintain serum calcium at satisfactory levels. That is why old people on limited diets can suffer from osteoporosis, a condition in which the bones become demineralised and weakened. Prevention of this condition should always be borne in mind. Ninety-nine percent of the calcium in the body is locked up in the bones. Here too it is the ratio which matters, in this case the ratio of calcium to phosphorus.

One of the main sources of calcium in the diet is dairy produce, notably cheese and milk, which are both relatively well-endowed with saturated animal fats. Other sources are whole fish, such as canned sardines and canned salmon, processed bread and flour (white bread contains more calcium than brown), cabbage, spinach and eggs. Top of the list, though, is seaweed . . .

Phosphorus
There is nearly a kilogram of phosphorus in the average adult body, most of it locked up in the bones and teeth in association with the calcium. The body needs about twice as much calcium as phosphorus and if this is not maintained then a compensating amount is removed from the bones to make up the difference. Unfortunately, much of our diet is now supplemented with hidden phosphorus. There are polyphosphates in meat products, there to retain water (selling which is more profitable, as the meat industry puts it, than selling meat), and in soft drinks, to give a sharp taste, there are compounds of phosphoric acid.

If this means that the body has adequate phosphorus, or even too much, and not enough calcium, then the calcium will be removed from the bones and osteoporosis will set in. In the USA, where added phosphorus is a significant item of the diet, osteoporosis can be seen in people as young as thirty who have a calcium-deficient, phosphorus-rich diet.

Important sources of phosphorus in the diet include cheese and eggs, meat and fish, brown bread (which contains more phosphorus than white) and vegetables. Canned drinks and processed meats can raise the amounts more than is healthy without a good supply of calcium. The perfect food, with a ratio of 2:1, is sauerkraut.

Magnesium

Like phosophorus, 70% of magnesium is found in the skeleton, and 30% in the soft tissue. Magnesium is concerned with the transmission of nerve signals and with the function of the muscles; in farm animals fed a diet that was lacking magnesium, tetanic spasm developed and the animals suffocated to death as their muscles ceased working. In humans, magnesium would be hard to avoid for it is abundantly present in green vegetables (where it is obtained from the chlorophyll in the leaves) and in cereals. There is about 25g magnesium in the average adult, about an ounce, and $1/3$ gram is reckoned to be the daily requirement.

Iron

'Enough iron to make half a pound of rusty nails' was the amount taught to children decades ago as the body's content of this element. There is about 4 g iron in the body, mainly tied up in the haemoglobin of the blood. Amounts that are needed per day are about 10mg in males and rather more in menstruating females. The amount lost by the body's metabolism is only about 1 mg, but absorption from the gut is not efficient and so extra is needed to compensate.

Iron is lost from a menstruating woman at a rate that is often not met by dietary intake, and iron-deficiency anaemia must be one of the most widespread diseases in Western society. There is extra iron in fortified bread, but iron salts tend to cause fats to become rancid and that can affect the shelf-life – and possibly the safety – of bakery goods. Iron in the form of the actual metal is now used in some areas, for this can be absorbed reasonably well if it is in the form of a very fine powder, and it has no deleterious effects on shelf-life.

The obvious answer would be to take extra iron just in case. But a small proportion of people have a condition called haemo-chromatosis which leads to damage to the liver cells if a high level of iron is taken in the diet. So a high 'background' of iron would be harmful to those patients, even if it helped rectify deficiencies in the rest of the population.

What are the levels concerned? For a male, around 10mg per day. For a woman, 18–20 mg. The level at which liver damage can appear in a victim of haemochromatosis is 40 mg per day. So an intake between 20 and 40 mg would clearly benefit everyone and cause danger to no one. In practice, most people take 10–20 mg in Westernised diets, which leaves a proportion of women somewhat anaemic. An additional 10mg a day in tablet form during the child-bearing years might be useful advice for women.

Iodine

This element, which everyone associates with seaweed as a dietary source, is needed in very small amounts, less than one-tenth milligram per day. It is vitally important for the proper functioning of the thyroid and a lack of iodine in the diet results in over-development of the thyroid gland. In Britain endemic goitre of this sort was called Derbyshire neck, since the water supplies in Derbyshire were deficient in iodine and the goitre appeared as a result. Iodate is sometimes used in bread, which can provide all you need in a day, and iodised table salt is sold too. One way to make up the deficit would be to add iodine to water, for this would control the disease – and goitre can kill if untreated. However, ethical considerations have always made that unacceptable, and iodised table salt is the preferred medium of administration, a comparison I shall explore when we turn to fluorine a little later. Overdosing with iodine occurs if more than about one milligram per day is taken in the diet, but most normal daily foodstuffs contain an amount that is within the required band of administration.

Zinc

The daily dose of zinc is reckoned to be around 10 mg for children and 15 mg for adults, and good sources are meat, offal, eggs and sea-food. There are small amounts in cereals too (about 0.5 mg per 100 mg cereal product) but the presence of fibre tends to hinder absorption. If about three-quarters of the recommended daily dose is present, the deficiency appears in the form of a loss of appetite and a first symptom may be hypogeusia – loss of the sense of taste.

Zinc is involved in many reactions concerning enzymes in the body; it helps the manufacture of the digestive juices (including

111

stomach acid, necessary for the first stages of digestion) and the breakdown of alcohol in the bloodstream. It is likely that the daily intake of zinc hovers around the required minimum, but some research workers have speculated that a proportion of us may be actually zinc-deficient. Supplements are available, but check how much they contain. One bulky-looking zinc tablet on the market only contains a milligram of metallic zinc and that would make only a small difference to the dietary intake.

Copper

Enzyme reactions in the body frequently depend on copper, and about 1–3 mg per day are required. Nuts are a good source, so are meat and liver. Diets that lack copper altogether are only known from experiments in the laboratory, but the results of absolute deficiency include degeneration of the nerves and skeleton, anaemia and failure of the reproductive organs. It may be that it is a lack of copper which is involved in marasmus, the starvation disease seen in underdeveloped nations, as well as a lack of actual food. There is always enough copper in a varied daily diet, but it has been claimed that excess vitamin C in the diet can act against the absorption of copper, and copper itself can cause fats to become rancid more readily.

Cobalt

A single atom of cobalt occurs in every molecule of vitamin B_{12} and it is necessary for the formation of the blood. Only a trace is required in the daily diet, and liver and meat are both adequately rich sources.

Chromium

A lack of chromium slows the growth rate, for this element is associated with the enzymes of glucose metabolism (and glucose is the body's first-line energy source). It occurs in meat as well as in yeast, so it can be found in beer and wine too.

No deficiency would normally be found, and the dose rate required in a day is easily met by the normal diet.

Fluorine

An adequate supply of fluorine in the diet is important for the health of teeth and bones, and reduced levels of fluorine are associated with raised levels of dental decay in children. Fluorine is present in sea fish and also in tea. It occurs in some areas in the water supply, and fluoridation has been widely recommended by dental authorities. Many of the arguments against fluoridation are irrational, for you would need to drink a month's supply of water in a single day to suffer from any side-effects.

But there is the ethical objection, and in my view fluoridation remains an unnecessary procedure. Goitre, as I have said, is a potentially life-threatening disease rectified by the sale of iodised table-salt. Now, if we do not seek to add iodine to water to intervene in a possibly lethal disease, we are in no position to put fluoride into water to control a much less serious condition.

Fluoridation cannot be 'mass medication'. Medications cure, and fluoridation does not cure anything; it is intended to *prevent* caries. But with the precedent of iodised table salt I see no reason why we should not prefer to administer fluorine to people who live in deficient areas through the sale of fluoridated toothpaste. This provides the right element in the right place at the regular intervals you would require, and does not transgress the ethical strictures established by our practice of administering iodine.

Manganese
Nuts, fruits, cereals and vegetables supply us with the 3 – 7 mg of manganese we require each day and deficiencies are not seen in normal circumstances. Traces of this element are important for the development of bone, and the enzymes of the nerves often include manganese.

Molybdenum
Peas and beans are our main source of this element, which has never been found to be deficient. Indeed it is so widespread in the normal diet that no account has been published of deficiency even in experimental animals. Enzyme reactions often require a trace of molybdenum, and about 200 mg per day are required.

Additional Trace Elements
Many other elements go into the body's processes and it is unlikely we will ever know the full extent of the varied reactions in which they play a part. Among these are selenium, usually obtained from wheat, which is involved with vitamin E metabolism; nickel, tin, vanadium and silicon, which seem to be mainly involved with enzyme reactions within the cells. Traces of other elements are poisonous, such as cadmium and lead. Strict controls are needed on these, and the banning of lead tetraethyl in petrol would be a significant step in the right direction.

The normal varied diet that most people eat supplies the majority of these elements without any problem. Those with specific dietary restrictions may require supplements, and some of the most important components of a diet are confined to animal-originated foods. Some are only found in plants. So, for people who wish to avoid one category or the other, advice would be a sensible precaution, so that dietary supplements could be taken if they became necessary. Simply leaving out all the meat and meat products from a previously omnivorous diet would be unwise; and similarly people who simply declare they no longer wish to eat fresh vegetables, or who give up all fruit (as can happen when people get older), will be liable to suffer from dietary deficiencies.

CHAPTER NINE

There have been many changes in recent years which have given us types of food, and shades of medical opinion, that would have seemed unimaginable a few decades ago. In Britain the most radical change has been in the provision of foods that are quick to prepare and which do not take too long to eat. Some of these are the recognisable fast foods, like hamburgers, whilst others are ethnic foodstuffs in the restaurants run by immigrant families and firms. The value of these foods in terms of their healthiness is often debated, but it would be wrong to conclude that food is necessarily 'bad' because it is 'fast'. The greatest problem lies in the impetus that seems to be driving us towards prepacked and prepared meals, eaten from trays held on the lap with the TV blaring away. There is a marketing advantage in coyly claiming that one is 'freeing people from drudgery' but we are also losing out on the pleasure of preparing family meals. And one can add 'saving time for what?' It is not as though people are busy in their spare time, for the main preoccupation is watching television programmes. There is a closer relationship between coronary heart disease statistics and watching TV than there is between coronary heart disease and saturated animal fat, or refined sugar. Not because TV causes heart attacks – it is, as I shall explain, because the life style of a sedentary and stressful Westerner is ill-matched to survival.

Currently the fast food business in Britain adds up to £2¼ billion per annum. This is divided as follows:

		Takeaway Proportion:
FISH AND CHIPS	£650m	80%
HAMBURGERS	£420m	37%
SANDWICHES	£420m	70%
CHINESE	£280m	80%
INDIAN	£190m	45%
CHICKEN	£160m	90%
PIZZA	£155m	25%

The growth in the hamburger business is shown by the staff employed by the McDonald organisation. In 1974 in the UK they had 60 workers. The numbers increased as follows: 1974 60: 1975 40: 1976 750: 1977 1,200: 1978 2,500: 1979 4,000: 1980 4,300: 1981 4,800: 1982 5,800: 1983 9,300. In ten scant years, from sixty persons employed to nearly ten thousand.

The expansion in this area is enormous. McDonald's spend almost £40m a year in expanding their franchise, and aim to put a McDonald's in every community in the UK that has a population big enough to make it viable. Wimpy's – which have become rather less fashionable under the onslaught of the American giants – plan to have 430 units in Britain in 1987. Huckleberry's doubled their outlets in 1984 alone, and were reportedly offering property agents the lure of a £1,000 holiday as an inducement to let them know of suitable sites for new operations. Pizzaland set a target of opening one new restaurant every ten days across the country. Kentucky Fried Chicken, with over 360 outlets, say they have been earmarked for rapid growth. At the present time industry is expanding at about 15% per annum, and there are over 20,000 fast food outlets in Britain.

It is not a licence to print money, though. The chain of Trumps shops lost over £2m before the owners, Bejam, sold it off to Grand Metropolitan, and the Hungry Fisherman chain was closed down too after it failed to show a reasonable profit. But the successful centres are big money-takers – revenue of £2,000 an hour has been reported from the best of the bunch, which is a high turnover for anyone. Pay is not very high, and many of the staff are youngsters without other alternatives, or students working spare-time.

How profitable is the business? Figures vary greatly, of course, but a representative breakdown of costs might be like this:

COST OF FOOD	50p
WAGES	28p
FRANCHISE FEE	10p
OPERATING COST	12p
RENT	8p
RATES	4p
VAT	20p
PROFIT	18p
COST OF BURGER TO CUSTOMER:	£1.50

There are two points that are worthy of special interest. One is that the profit here is quite small, relatively speaking; restaurants (which are greatly overpriced in Britain as a matter of tradition) have a very much greater mark-up than this. The other is that – small profit or no – the cost of the burger you buy is three times the cost of the food from which it is made. That loading on costs, compared with the pleasures of putting a meal together at home, is considerable.

Yet people probably do not realise what they are eating. The milk shake in a burger bar may look pretty innocuous alongside the greasy chips and the hamburger itself, but the chips contain less fat than the burger, whilst the milk-shake contains half as much as the fattening-looking chips! (McDonald's figures show: 12.1g fat in the milkshake; less than double that, 21.3g, in the french fries, compared with 27.9g in the burger.) People often decline to take the large portion of french fries (containing, say McDonald, 386 calories) and settle instead for the milk shake (380 calories – virtually the same calorie count!).

You will note that I have avoided the term 'beefburger' in the above descriptions. Technically, no such thing exists. The common assumption that hamburger has something to do with 'ham' is erroneous. The word arose from the town of Hamburg, where chopped and reformed steak is popularly believed to have begun; and so a hamburger is meant to be made from beef. The original recipe is close to that for the raw steak tartare, and in its original form a hamburger may have been a lightly grilled tartare steak. Meats (like the wursts of Germany) are often eaten in Europe with bread, which is where the hot-dog originated; and the American craze for hamburgers and hot-dogs in Europe is essentially a re-importation (in modified form) of a way of eating taken across the Atlantic by European émigrés.

People buy a tremendous number of preformed hamburgers from freezer centres, though making them at home is much more satisfying and takes next to no time. Many of the commercially available products are rich in added ingredients, which may be a few extra flavourings (not listed under the E numbers scheme) or in some cases a considerable bulk of cereals and onion.

My recommendation to mince your own meat, if you wish to eat hamburger steaks, is based on the fact that the content of minced meat from butchers' shops is very variable, and often contains larger amounts of fat than you might expect. A far-reaching survey by the Association of Public Analysts in Britain showed that 3,500 minced meat samples averaged about 16 per cent fat, which is actually quite low. There is hidden fat in meat, which is partly responsible for the taste of a meaty dish, and some will remain even if all the excess visible external fat is carefully cut away. The problems lie in the honesty of your butcher. The leanest sample in that survey contained a mere 9% fat, and was, very fittingly, labelled BEST LEAN MINCE. But, on the other hand, the most fatty sample of all – rated at 26% fat – was labelled ENGLISH BEEF LEAN MINCE.

It seemed that the butchers who simply sold 'mince' rated about 17% average fat in the samples. Those who had labels of quality reading 'best' or 'lean' were either high-quality reputable butchers who were determined to provide the best for their customers, or unscrupulous people selling sub-standard minced meat who were determined to bluff it out. Though legally acceptable minimum standards have not been set for minced meat, prosecutions have been successfully carried out in cases where butchers had sold meat containing more than 25% fat as 'mince'. The best answer would be for a butcher to display the maximum content of fat in his product, though that might be difficult for him (or you) to control. Until an easy means of measuring fat content is intro-duced, the most sensible solution is to buy your meat from a butcher you have grown to trust. But, like sausages, the amount of fat that runs out when you cook the product on its own can sometimes give you a shocking information of just how much fat there really is.

Sausages in Europe have to be made of meat, but in Britain they contain cereals and expanders, together with a generally unadmitted amount of fat. British sausages cannot be sold in mainland Europe as 'sausages' at all, for this reason. At home they remain very popular – we spend over £400m a year eating 6,000,000,000,000, sausages, according to one recent survey which many people have quoted, though these figures mean that a single pound of sausages would cost a fraction of a penny. I do hope people do not take statistics too seriously!*

Easier to measure is the content of sausages. And, as in the case of minced meat, content is reflected neither in price nor in description. The highest price in a 1984 survey was £2.20, and they contained 31% fat and 12% rusk, whilst the cheapest was 85p per lb, containing 30% fat and 10% rusk. The highest proportion of meat was 67%, with a mere 5% rusk, and those sold for £1.85. Some commercial producers now label their products with the proportions of ingredients, and this is the only safeguard you have in the average supermarket. But the trust you have for your butcher gives you the real answer to find a good source of meaty sausages for the family, if that is what they like to eat. Sausages can be made at home too, and kits with sausage skins are available for the enthusiast. Everyone should make sausages for themselves once in a while, rather than always buying the ready-made article from a shop.

The problem with sausages is what is actually meant by 'meat'. People assume that meat is the red food that you see displayed at the butcher's shop. Meat, according to our personal definitions, is the counterpoint to skin, or bone, or gristle, or fat. Not according to the trade. Here, the definition of meat really means anything but bone. It includes fat, skin, rind, gristle, sinew, all finely ground. The undesirable bits and pieces of animals go into sausage meat. That in itself should not cause anybody aesthetic problems. Eating them is not any different to eating other parts of an animal, and if you are repelled by the idea of consuming eyeballs and navels, as it were, then you should not be eating meat in the first instance.

The regulations that govern the content of a sausage in the UK

_____

*The actual number is about six thousand million, for the record.

119

state that (for beef sausages, as an example) 65% must be meat. But half of it need be 'lean meat' and, of that, ten percent can be fat. So, in the final sausage, 65% x 2 = 32.5% x 90% = 29% need be offcuts (including head-meat). A legal pork sausage can be 32% fat, 20% water, 10% rusk, 6% rind, 5% seasoning, preservative and colourant, and 27% off-cuts. Pork sausages are subjected to special regulations, since they must contain 65% meat – but, of that, 80% has to be pork. Even so, the actual pork meat in a pork sausage can be a very small proportion of the final product.

A pork pie weighing over 100g need contain no more than 19% meat, of which the lean meat need only be 50%. In round figures, this means one-tenth of a pork pie is pork in the sense in which you would recognise it. A half-pound pie need have no more than about 1½ *ounces* of pork. The remainder can contain small and large intestine, rectum and stomach, brain, foot and head, lungs and oesophagus, spinal cord, udder, testicles and spleen. Once again there is a case to be made out for making your own pork pie with chopped belly-pork. At least you can then savour the real delights of a pie that is flavoured by what it is supposed to contain, rather than by containing some surprising portions of the animal.

It is labelling which enables us to get to grips with what is contained in foods we buy, and many of the proposals over food labelling can be criticised for being inappropriate for people's needs. The most basic item of information for which people often look is the amount of energy the food confers on the consumer. Calories are themselves a source of confusion. In the first instance, a calorie is a meaninglessly small unit of energy and in practice a thousand calories are lumped together as a kilocalorie, often spelt as Calorie. From this you will realise that a calorie is a thousand times smaller than a Calorie, but in normal use the larger version – the kilocalorie, more correctly abbreviated to kcal – is what we mean by a 'calorie' and it usually has a small initial letter anyway. So the most widespread energy unit of all is not what it seems to be.

Worse than that, it is now being replaced by the kiloJoule, kJ. It is a kind of scientific pedantry which has forced this perfectly meaningless change on the food industry, and in fairness people are resisting it. Manufacturers who are required (or who volunteer) to give energy equivalents for their foodstuffs on packets usually print both units together, thus: 272 kJ/65 kcal and you can perform calculations easily enough if you bear in mind that a kiloJoule is a little more than four times the equivalent of a calorie (or Calorie (or kilocalorie).)

The European regulations on the labelling of foods now mean that there is certain information which *must* appear on the wrapper:

- The name of the food
- The net quantity
- Ingredients (in order of their abundance), datemark
- Manufacturer's name (or that of packer, or wholesaler).

There are other items which appear if appropriate:

- Instructions for use
- Special conditions for storage or application
- Country of origin if necessary.

The name of the food can cause problems, for people have set ideas about specific foods and what is, say, Scotch Broth to one person might be nothing of the sort to someone else. Quantity contained is a second problem for the consumer. In the pre-metric days, Britain had settled very well into a convention where cans contained a pint or a half-pint, a pound or a half-pound; since metrication the amounts of food in a tin can vary by a few grams from one maker to the next, until in a single kind of food you can find a huge array of different weights and volumes in similar-looking containers. All this makes comparative pricing impossible.

Ingredients can be confusing too. The listing of ingredients in their order of abundance in the food can helpfully show us that one of the main ingredients in a packet soup is salt, for example, but if you have three main ingredients taking up 30% each of the final weight, and then three more, each of them about 3%, the listing in order tends to make you feel that the proportions are more or less evenly spaced down a descending scale, rather than (as is the case here) in two main groups.

Datemarking is something else that causes problems. I helped campaign for some system of showing how old a food is, but it is not so easy in practice. Firstly, the conditions of storage can mean that a food that is over-date could easily be in a much safer condition than something still with weeks to go that had been kept under worse storage conditions. The stipulations for the datemark depend on how long the food lasts. If it is intended to last more than 18 months it needs no mark at all, but if a date does appear it should show a best-before date and an indication, if appropriate, of storage conditions.

A food that lasts 3–18 months should have a best-before date (month and year); a food intended to last 6–12 weeks should show day and month, plus storage conditions (if necessary), and a perishable food with less than 6 weeks' shelf-life should have the day and month of a sell-by date, plus storage conditions, plus an indication of the period of storage after purchase.

Not all foods need labels of this sort, among them wines and vinegar, honey, chocolate products, eggs, dried milk and food prepared at home for charitable sale. In addition, a wrapper measuring less than ten square centimetres in area need show nothing but the food name and (if appropriate) a datemark.

Even so, some of the descriptions can be misleading. For example, raspberry yoghurt must contain raspberries. Raspberry-flavoured yoghurt (meaning 'flavoured with raspberries') must contain the fruit too, and what is more the fruit must be the main source of the flavour. But something that says raspberry flavour need have been nowhere near the real fruit, but be flavoured with the biochemical products which convey the taste of the fruit.

Not all the ingredients are given in sufficiently clear form. Sugar is normally included under the generic term of 'carbohydrate'. Puffed wheat and Mars bars have both a similar carbohydrate content of two-thirds, for example. But the amount of carbohydrate that is sugar is rather more than 1% for the cereal, whilst it is 66% for the confection.

The content of wines and other alcoholic drinks is something that might deter the casual drinker, and no doubt that is why they are omitted. Here is an example:

TREATMENTS FOR WINE
Dried blood powder, isinglass, sturgeon's bladder, potassium ferro-cyanide, casein, egg white, gelatine, bentinite, silica dioxide, tannin, kaolin, acacia gum, charcoal. (The egg white and blood powder are used to coagulate last remaining residues of yeast so that they can be removed. The charcoal is applied to white wines to adsorb the colour of impurities, and the wines may be filtered and centrifuged to remove extraneous yeast, etc.)

Additives for Wine

Potassium tartrate, bicarbonate, bitratrate; calcium carbonate, copper sulphate; citric, tartaric or sorbic acids; ammonium phosphate and sulphate; thiamin, sugar and concentrated grape must, dioxides of sulphur and carbon, and water. (These are often used to improve the flavour or the alcoholic content, to control dissolved solids, to add sparkle,etc.) In addition a certain proportion of non-vintage or non-appellation wines may be added even to wines of a declared origin, in order to balance the flavour. So even here you may not get what you expect. In particular note the existence of some 'vins de fruits' which are not even made exclusively with grape juice. Some of these are sold as sparkling wines (and in fact can have a flavour better than that of a cheap and undistinguished champagne).

How much should you drink? Data do suggest that people who drink a certain amount of alcoholic beverages (wine or beer, depending on which authority you consider) are healthier, on average, than those who don't. It may even be that there is a positive correlationship between drink in small amounts and immunity to coronary heart disease. On the other hand, alcohol can damage the brain and the liver in susceptible people, and in anyone who drinks to excess. The safest way to assess how much you drink is to centre the mind on a basic drink. That equals a small spirit measure (e.g. a single gin or whisky), *or* a goblet of wine, *or* a small glass of sherry, *or* a measure of fortified wine. That is equivalent to half a pint of beer. So a double scotch is equivalent to a pint of bitter on that basis.

A good guide to drinking alcohol is that on average you should not drink more than, say, every other day; and that you should not regularly drink more than half a dozen basic drinks at a session (e.g. three pints of beer or six gins). On that level drinking is a social matter and not a cause for any concern. But two points: women have a lower threshold than men, and react quicker to alcohol. Part of this is because women are about 50% water, whilst men are more like 60% water, so the alcohol has 'less volume in which to spread'. Women are also more liable to liver damage from alcohol. And the second point is that a regular daily intake equivalent to 8–10 basic drinks a day – less for women, about 6–7 – puts you at the level where you may do yourself long-term harm. Alcohol is one of the items of our daily diet about which there is a clear cause-and-effect relationship between it and disease. It is not a matter of scholarly debate, nor is there any switch in fashion which may make alcohol harmless even in excess.

One recent target of interest in the dietary field may have applications in the treatment of alcoholism and the effects it has on the brain. This is gamma-linoleic acid, more conveniently known as GLA. One of the essential fatty acids is linoleic acid, which is abundant in some plant oils. This is converted into a form that the body can use – GLA – by action of enzymes which are very sensitive and which seem to be inhibited by saturated fats. So the idea has arisen of consuming the GLA in ready-made form, by-passing the possible bottleneck caused by a breakdown of the enzyme pathway.

One important source of GLA is the oil of *Oenothera*, the evening primrose. An even more concentrated form comes from *Borago*, the borage, and this plant is – like *Oenothera* – now being introduced as a non-food farming crop as the industry marketing GLA increases in size and scope. One function of GLA is the maintenance of the fatty structural components within the cells, and alcoholism is one of the conditions on which GLA is being used – apparently with some success. Some researchers suggest that the effect of alcohol is literally to dissolve away part of the insulating layers around the nerve cords in the brain, and for this reason they have applied GLA in an attempt to rectify the damage.

Initial research in Scotland and Ireland has suggested that GLA may indeed be of value in treating alcoholics. It also seems to help in the management of pre-menstrual tension, and it is being quoted as a dietary supplement which is of value in topping up the normal metabolic cycles. How true this is remains to be seen, but there can be no harm in adding some additional essential fatty acids to the diet. Certainly GLA is a current fashion. How much it has to support it remains to be seen.

Looking to the future for food processing, we already have a range of techniques for freezing, drying, canning; and these should be respected for their special applications. Freezing is probably less attractive than the fashionable view would suggest. The action of freezing bursts plant cell walls and causes a breakdown of structure – to some extent – in most foods. Frozen foods are always liable to lose texture because of it. The idea of keeping a well stocked freezer is not the godsend it might seem: there are maintenance and breakdown costs, the electricity or gas is an additional cost, for the system relies on the continual pumping out of heat energy day and night; and the food can be difficult to use rationally (it is often hard to find what you want in a crowded freezer compartment). The best way to obtain fresh and crisp vegetables is to grow them yourself, and since this is not possible for many people then buy them fresh whenever possible. It can be a mistake to keep vegetables in a refrigerator, for they are destined to become limp and listless even in the crisper compartment – so-called – of a domestic fridge. The best way to keep vegetables lively and crisp is to stand them in water on a bright window-sill. Broccoli will revive and become plump and crisp, and cabbage will swell out and become alive again. Then – when cooked with a little briskly boiling water, or for a short time in a pressure-cooker – you can taste fresh vegetables. They are greatly superior to what you would find in a freezer.

Dried foods are rarely used these days, apart from herbs and dried fruit (raisins, currants, etc). But canned food – unlike frozen – probably has a *worse* image than it deserves. The principle of cooking food is to use a short time whenever you can, and in the factory that produces canned food the cooking process matches this ideal very well. The food you find in a can is in essence fresh-cooked and it compares well with restaurant cooking at its best. An added advantage is that the food is sealed, so there is no chance of spoilage, of strange odours being absorbed, and what is more there is no requirement for energy input in order to keep the food in that state. It will stay in its can, fresh-cooked and out of contact with damaging outside agencies, until you wish to use it. It can last for decades like this, though most canned foods are more sensibly consumed within a year.

These comments about frozen and canned goods may help to balance the fashionable passions of our age. Both have their good points, and their bad; but the popularity of frozen foods over canned has little to support it.

What of the future?

There remains one additional means of preserving food that we may see further developed – the irradiation of food. In this technique, food in a sealed container is passed through a beam of gamma rays in order to sterilise it. Microbes in the food are destroyed. The food then remains in a fresh state, at least free from microbe degradation, until the pack is opened. A second use of gamma rays is to prevent crops from germinating in storage.

The rays prevent the cells from dividing, and potatoes will remain unsprouting in store during trans-shipment, for example.

The first approval of gamma rays in food was in the USSR as long ago as 1958, where it was applied to potatoes as described above. Within ten years of that date the concept had been approved in Canada and the USA, also Israel; and the next year added the Netherlands, Spain and Hungary. In each case the foods were processed in plants essentially made for industrial purposes, and the first purpose-built plant for food was erected in Japan in 1974. The isotope that provides the rays is cobalt–60, kept in lead-lined rooms at the bottom of a tank of water. The goods are wheeled in on pallets, the room closed, and then the cobalt–60 source is raised for a set time to irradiate the food. During this time it sterilises the consignment and then the cobalt–60 is lowered again into its watery container, after which the room is opened and the pallets removed.

Popular conceptions of the term 'radiation' and of 'irradiated food' are fashionably negative. For this reason, although more and more approval has been given around the world, Britain has been reluctant to sanction it. The dangers of radiation in food are extremely remote. Residual radiation is no objection, and the processing of food through a radiation chamber does less to alter the food than, say, cooking. The food remains in an identical state to its original condition, apart from the fact that organisms are destroyed and the food rendered sterile. The microbes that contaminate foods at present cause a significant hazard to human health and it is unfortunate that the traditional distaste of anything to do with radiation has prevented us from adopting this safe and remarkably efficient means of making food safe in the future.

For the future, then, food is going to become more international. We have recognised our ability to produce food on a huge scale, and there is currently no shortage of protein for the world population. The fact that we continue to support lakes of drink and mountains of food as a result of political theories that subsidise farmers to produce foodstuffs we cannot consume, yet which do not extend to passing them to societies which need them urgently, is a matter of which history should make us ashamed. Equally interesting is the fact that nations which support large populations of starving peasant people still find themselves able also to support internecine wars waged for political reasons, rather than attending to the plight of the people they represent. Such matters are beyond the scope of a survey of foodstuffs, but it is sensible to remind ourselves of the fact that our own style of life is not typical of that found around the world. Our own conditions for living are elevated beyond the dreams of two-thirds of our fellows, and the fact that we are now facing a future where we should cut down on how much we eat, and become less wasteful in our attitudes to food, fits strangely into such a context. Science has done so much to improve our lot, yet so little to enable us to understand our context in world affairs. The present existence of vast amounts of excess production is a moral problem as much as a physical or economic one. Easy solutions do not work. The simple answer is to suggest that we find starving people in the less developed countries and feed them with the food. That saves lives on the point of extinction, but merely moves the problem back to the next bottleneck. Indeed it may not work at all, for the kind of food we have available may not be the kind the deprived peoples need, or can eat. However, if you were to give a community a supply of free food you would immediately undermine the slender economy and trading structure of the region and disrupt the community structure. At least, that is the argument used against the idea by politicos.

That is all very well in a 'free market economy', but in Britain and the rest of Europe we have no such thing, in spite of the protestations of government. We control by strict government limits such things as salaries for nurses and teachers, costs of energy for the old (natural gas could be far less expensive if it were not pegged to the oil rate – and fluctuations in the oil price show how true that is) and the price of foods bought on the intervention market, such as milk, butter and grain.

We should be able to offer foods on a heavily subsidised basis, say, as part of an aid budget; we should be able to expand the rate at which we buy produce back from a stricken nation at preferential rates (we do it for our own farmers). Then surplus foods could enter the country's economy with little cost to the gross national product, and would re-fuel the indigenous economy. The incentives to re-establish an active system of commercialism, which is the aim for which bureaucracies reach, would be considerable and we would avoid the risk of saturating a stagnant economy and destroying its capacity to expand.

The present tendency of recognising overproduction and so cutting back on food production is immoral in a starving world. It may work for Britain, even for Europe, if that is what you conceive of as the community. But I would hope we would now see the global community as the structure that matters, and to which we owe our allegiance. There have been cases of families in which the children have been starved, whilst the adults obtained all they needed to eat; cases in which the parents have been gaoled and heavily censured by that community. How strange it is that we can sanction exactly that attitude when the adults and the starving are separated by a conveniently large distance. I would have imagined that the same criteria would apply, though it seems I am wrong in that supposition.

CHAPTER TEN

And so the ultimate remedy: dieting. The surveys suggest that currently half of women in the UK and the USA are dieting, and the proportion of men is steadily nearing that total. There have been many diets to choose from, and many ways in which to observe them. Yet little has been said on the principles that lie behind dieting programmes. The criteria by which we select our actions are themselves a little-explored area, and in the food field they become intricate and revealing. Little is known about the reasons that encourage people to stop eating enough, often until their survival is threatened. The condition is known as *anorexia nervosa*, and the fact that it manifests itself as a single, visible symptom (slow starvation) tends to make us think of it as a single disease with a single cause. There are many reasons why a person should undertake such a form of self-destruction. It could be revenge, dissatisfaction, frustration, cruelty, a brain disease, a biochemical disorder or a learned code of behavioural criteria . . . there may be many reasons that trigger the single response.

The trigger behind obesity is complex too. I have suggested that the exact level of your weight is inwardly programmed through an adipostat, and the fact that people – some people – can eat a vast amount of food and never put on an ounce is testimony to the fact that your equilibrium is inwardly set. The overeating that causes fatness in some does not in others, and there is no argument with that.

But why does a person who has a tendency to become fat

suddenly allow matters to get out of hand, putting on weight which they themselves find unattractive and debilitating? The dieting organisations which provide plans of action for those who need this kind of discipline say that a woman is 'punishing herself' by allowing herself to become fat. Her health suffers, her morale sinks, her personal habits deteriorate, they warn; she is becoming a masochist.

I doubt this. There is another factor at work. She is not just punishing herself, but punishing her family. She removes from them her attractiveness, adds to their own burdens by the worry they may experience if she seems to be losing her health. At the same time she has a subtle revenge – she is indulging herself in foods she loves, she is spending on her own whims and fancies. It is a fact that modern families in which both parents work (and this is a trend reinforced by economic strictures and encouraged by governments) still expect mother to do the housework, to take responsibility for organising the home comforts, and yet give little in response. Words of appreciation seem to be rare these days, and even the expression of thanks for a meal are uncommon. Little wonder women may be disinclined to work for their families, when there is so little reason to do so and such limited appreciation at the end of the day.

The overeating by an exploited mother who has a tendency to become fat is a form of revenge. She loves it, and makes herself unavailable to the parasites at home by the withdrawal of the attractive person she might otherwise have been.

Starting a diet is hindered by several factors. In primitive times humans ate food until they were no longer hungry. Now they eat food until they feel full. The reason for that is the flavour enhancement that modern techniques provide. There is a continued tendency for us to eat to excess. Dieting is also hindered by our desire for routine. We eat regular meals at regular times, and frequently they are composed of similar items from meal to meal. We did not evolve in such a structured life-style, and the fact that our bodies are waiting for food at the appointed hour is further encouragement to eat more than we need. For those of us with a 'high setting' on the adipostat there are several reasons why we should put on weight.

Working out a low-calorie diet is made more difficult than it need be by the complexity of the calculations. The energy calculation tables show how many calories there are in food. To work out what you are eating, you have to work out how much the food weighs, and then multiply that by the number of calories per unit weight, all of which leads to confusion and takes much of the fun out of the meal. A better way to tackle this is proposed in the table – it reverses the process. Rather than showing the calories in a set weight of food, it shows the weight of food that gives you a set number of calories, in this case 100 calories. It is easy to cut a given weight of food, within reasonable limits, and I propose it would be easy for food retailers to sell food, not just by weight, but in 100 calorie portions (or some other multiple). It would make dieting very easy indeed and be an immediate indicator of how much food energy you were consuming.

How Much Food Can You Eat?

The normal energy tables show how many calories there are in your food. This shows the opposite – namely, how much food provides the same amount of calories. A range of common foods are shown, and in each case the weight that supplies 100 calories is shown. The totals are approximate, and have been double-checked. Cutting food to a specified weight, and then calculating how many calories it contains, is a time-consuming business. This new alternative makes the task of dieting very much similar. An ounce roughly equals 30 grams.

All-bran cereal 1½ oz
Alpen cereal 1 oz
Angel delight 2½ oz
Apple 6½ oz
Avocado 4 oz
Bacon 1½ oz
(grilled 1 oz
(fried ¾ oz
Banana 5 oz
Bean sprouts 34 oz
Beans (baked) 3½ oz
Beef 1½
Beetroot 6½ oz
Biscuits (about) ½ oz
Blackberries 10 oz

Muesli 1 oz
Mustard and cress 35 oz
Oil (cooking) ⅓ oz
Outline 1 oz
Oxo cubes 2 oz
Parsley 20 oz
Pâté (less than) 1 oz
Pasta 1 oz
Peanuts (about) 1½ oz
Pear 10 oz
Peas 3 oz
Peppers (sweet) 25 oz
Pickles 2–4 oz
Pies (about) 1½ oz
Pilchards 2 oz

Bran 1 oz

Brandy ¾ oz

Bread 1½ oz (= 2 thin slices)

Brussels sprouts 20 oz

Buns (about) 1 oz

Butter ½ oz

Cabbage 20 oz

Cake (about) 1 oz

Carrots 20 oz

Cauliflower 33 oz

Celery 50 oz

Cereals (about) 1 oz

Cheese (about) 1 oz

Cheesecake ⅔ oz

Chicken 2 oz

Chips 1½ oz

Chocolate (about) ⅔ oz

Christmas pudding 1 oz

Cider 10 oz

Cole slaw 2 oz

Corn on cob 3 oz

Corned beef 1½ oz

Cornish pasty 1 oz

Cream (about) 1 oz

Cress 20 oz

Crispbread 1 oz

Croissant 1 oz

Cucumber 34 oz

Curry 2–3 oz

Doughnuts 1 oz

Duck 1 oz

Dumplings 1½ oz

Egg (whole) 2 oz

Egg white 10 oz

Egg yolk 1 oz

Fish 1–2 oz

Flour 1 oz

Frankfurter 1½ oz

Gateau 1 oz

Gherkins 100 oz

Gin 1½ oz

Pizza 1½ oz

Pineapple 10 oz

Pork pie 1 oz

Porridge, cooked, 6½ oz

Potato 3 oz

Potato crisps ⅔ oz

Potato salad 2 oz

Puffed wheat 1 oz

Quiche 1 oz

Rabbit 2 oz

Radish 25 oz

Raisin bran 1 oz

Rarebit, welsh, 1 oz

Ravioli 3 oz

Rhubarb 100 oz

Rice (boiled) 3 oz

Rice Krispies 1 oz

Rissoles 1½ oz

Ritz crackers ⅔ oz

Roe 1½ oz

Rolls 1½ oz

Rusks 1 oz

Ryvita 1 oz

Salad cream 1 oz

Salami (less than) 1 oz

Salmon 2 oz

Sauces (about) 1–2 oz

Sauerkraut 20 oz

Sausages 1¼ oz

(1 sausage = about 2 oz)

Scones 1 oz

Seakale 50 oz

Shellfish 5 oz

Sherbert 1 oz

Shredded wheat (less than) 1 oz

Slimca bread 1½ oz

Smarties ¾ oz

Spinach 20 oz

Squid 4 oz

Steak 1½ oz

Strawberries 20 oz

Grapes 5 oz
Grapefruit (fresh) 34 oz
Grapefruit (canned) 5 oz
Haggis 2 oz
Hamburger 1½ oz
Hot dog sausage 1½ oz
Jam 1½ oz
Ketchup 3 oz
Kidney 2 oz
Kippers 1½ oz
Kit Kat ²/₃ oz
Lamb (about) 2 oz
Lard ¹/₃ oz
Leek 20 oz
Lemon 20 oz
Lettuce 35 oz
Liver 1½ oz
Lobster 3 oz
Margarine (about) ½ oz
Marrow 100 oz
Marzipan (less than) 1 oz
Mayonnaise 1 oz
Meat 1 2 oz
Melon 20 oz
Milk 5 oz
Milk, skimmed, 10 oz
Mincemeat 3 oz

Stuffing 1 oz
Sucron 4 oz
Suet pudding 1 oz
Sugar 1 oz
Swede 20 oz
Sweet 'n' low 1 oz
Syrup 1 oz
Tangarines 10 oz
Tea 100 oz
Toad-in-hole 1½ oz
Tomato 25 oz
Tongue 1½ oz
Trifle 2 oz
Tripe 3 oz
Trout 2½ oz
Tuna 1½ oz
Turkey 2 oz
Turkish Delight 1 oz
Twix bar ²/₃ oz
Vita Wheat ¾ oz
Waistline dressing 2 oz
Watercress 20 oz
Weetabix 1 oz
Yeast (dry) 1 oz
Yorkshire pudding 1½ oz
Zabaione ½ oz

The most drastic methods of losing weight involve the intervention of surgeons. The intestine can be short-circuited so that the area available for the absorption of food is greatly reduced. In this operation, jejunal-ileal bypass surgery, the length of time the food stays in the small intestine is shorter and the patient takes in far less nourishment than before. There are some potential problems through the lowering of nutriments taken in – care has to be taken to avoid malnutrition since it is all the valuable foodstuffs that are being subjected to reduced absorption, and not merely the calorific component. Some reports have suggested that cirrhosis of the liver can occur as a result of this operation, appearing after a few years. On the other hand, the operation is theoretically reversible (the loops of intestine are not removed, merely short-circuited, so they could be reinstated if the need arose). All operations have a hazard attached to them, and it has been claimed that jejunal-ileal bypass has a mortality as high as five percent. If that is so, it would seem a high price to pay for the goal of losing weight, especially when that can be obtained in practice without any need for surgery.

A practical disadvantage of the operation is that a proportion of the patients pass several liquid stools a day, which is inconvenient. It seems that the amount of weight lost by this operation is actually more than can be explained away by the loss of intestinal aborptive area, and that may be because people have to eat smaller amounts than normal in order to feel comfortable.

Less severe in its implications is the stapling of the stomach to make its volume smaller. The stomach is given a new volume only ten percent of its former size, and this means that large amounts of food cannot be retained at once. The patient takes far smaller meals at a sitting as there is no room for the food. Although the operation is less drastic (no organs are actually taken out of circulation in this approach) the surgery is more difficult and the mortality rate is a little higher than in the jejunal-ileal bypass alternative. And here, too, the smaller amounts of food could be eaten by conscious decision of the patient, rather than through surgical intervention.

A direct way of losing fat is its removal from the body. There have been attempts to liquefy the fat and draw it off, though the most widely used approach is the technique of apronectomy, in which the abdomen is opened and layers of fatty tissue neatly excised with the scalpel. A neat scar, normally hardly noticeable, is left and the patient has meanwhile lost several pounds of redundant fatty tissue. For fat people who have a need to lose weight, this is a form of surgery which is at least justifiable, whereas the earlier alternatives are harder to support.

The fourth way in which doctors can surgically intervene is through jaw splinting. The upper and lower jaws are wired together, so that the patient can no longer eat. Nutriments now have to be taken through a straw, in liquid form. It is true that some compulsive eaters have lost weight impressively through this form of intervention, but others have continued to gain weight by obsessive consumption of highly calorific liquidised foodstuffs. The eating of food to great excess, as is the case in people who need this treatment, is essentially a personal problem, and the masochistic overtones of having one's mouth wired shut do little to solve psychological problems in the broader sense. If they are at the core of the over-eater's problem in any particular case, then the jaw splinting will not be a long-term solution. But, as in the earlier examples of intervention by doctors, close supervision of the patient is necessary. Sceptics might point to the vested interests that some doctors have in working in this essentially cost-effective field, but if people wish to lose weight and these are the only means that they can see working, then surgery is arguably better than nothing.

Doctors can also use drugs to depress the appetite. The classic drug for this purpose was amphetamine, which also turns out to be a stimulant with an addictive (or at least habituating) propensity. Other appetite depressants are on sale, one of which was previously marketed as being capable of literally 'metabolising fat', though that claim has since been abandoned. There is currently some research effort into modifying the amphetamine molecule so that the product still acts against the appetite, whilst having a lowered tendency to cause habituation.

The greatest focus of attention has, for decades, centred on the fad diets. Books on diets which catch the attention of the media always make a tidy fortune for their authors, they always attract thousands of adherents, they become the talking point of every party, they dominate every newspaper feature column and ooze from the television programmes. Then they are discredited, the fashions change, the books go to the jumble sale, and the adherents put back whatever weight they lost at the time.

Most of these diets do work, in the sense that they cause followers to lose weight. If this happens, it is because food intake has fallen below the daily requirement for energy. But the way the diets fail is in aiming for this in a way that is questionable. They are usually based on some fragment of scientific wisdom expanded to ludicrous lengths, and many of them have loopholes.

One example, now lost in the obscurity of the decades, was the 'inches-off diet'. The concept was to restrict protein, presumably so that fat reserves would be broken down instead. This was obtained by leaving out the highly proteinaceous components of the diet – meat and poultry, fish, eggs, milk and cheese, nuts and pulses. The diet was widely claimed to enable women (not men, note) to remove excess weight precisely where they wanted to lose it. The claim is dubious, and so is the diet if a healthy form of eating is your aim. Many important amino acids and vitamins are

135

lost in such a profound restriction of protein foods, and weight loss is brought about by unhealthy means.

An example of a diet that worked by restriction of the overall food intake was the 'Hollywood 18' diet which stipulated that nothing but grapefruit and lamb chops should be eaten for eighteen days at a time. No ban on protein here, you note but the limited intake of food cannot claim to give a healthy mixed diet. In fact lamb is one of the foods to which people are least likely to become allergic, so this diet might have worked for people who wished to track down an allergy to some item of their daily food intake. The 'Hollywood 18' diet worked by providing a monotonous diet which could not be transgressed, so it was easy to follow for the obsessively inclined.

Other diets have advised the restriction, not of protein, but of carbohydrate. It is from this rationale that the ban on bread and potatoes arose. Low carbohydrate diets were first advised in the mid–1800s, and they are claimed to work by the simple expedient of supplying so little energy from carbohydrate that fats *have* to be burned as an energy source instead. Here is a classic example of a little scientific finding being expanded into a whole dietary principle. The metabolism of the body depends on a good balance between fats and carbohydrates, and the lack of carbohydrate leads to the production of ketosis, an abnormal state in which compounds like acetone appear in the bloodstream. One of these diets, the Stillman diet, states you should drink several pints of water a day in order to wash these ketone bodies out of the blood and carry them into the urine. Another version, the Atkins diet, does not insist on ridding the body of ketones, but rather seeks to identify them as an indication that the diet is working regularly. Ketone test strips (as used by diabetics) are supplied to these dieters, so that they can test their own urine and monitor the presence of ketones. If the test is positive, then a state of ketosis exists and that, says the dietary school, shows that fats are being metabolised. There are many reported long-term effects of this approach, including allegations of gout, osteoporosis and cardiac irregularities. In addition, people taking low-carbohydrate diets usually end up consuming far more fats than normal, because the diet is inherently unbalanced.

The most unbalanced diet of all must be the macrobiotic concept. This moves through phases of restriction until a final plateau is reached in which the only food is brown rice. The diet has been associated with claims that followers would realise their fondest dreams, and that the idea could cure all illness (including those not yet developed by the individual dieter)! Fatalities have been associated with this strict regime, which is deficient in many essential nutriments and is unlike anything with which our species has had contact in the past. It is a profoundly unnatural diet, far more so than the worst excesses of today's hi-tech diets.

Other diets have been idiosyncratic, rather than frankly hazardous. The Mayo diet was one; it had no connection with the famous Mayo Clinic (which regularly issued disclaimers) and seemed to be based on the eating of grapefruit before each meal. This, it was claimed, contained enzymes which led to the dissipation of fat. That claim would be incorrect, for no such enzymes could be absorbed by the body (any present would be inactivated by the acid digestion of the stomach). The diet seemed to suppress appetite by presenting this astringent food – grapefruit – before anything else was eaten. The bacon and eggs that most people ate after their fruit as part of the Mayo diet supplied other vital nutrients, but were very high in saturated animal fats, cholesterol, and salt. None of those would pass muster in the light of today's fashionable views.

There was even the Humplik diet, which claimed that some foods have a negative calorific value. According to this idea, some items in the diet use up more energy in the process of being digested than they themselves originally contained. One example quoted was that an egg contained an energy equivalent of 80 calories, but took 92 calories to be digested. The net difference of 12 calories was a loss of energy from the body. According to this, the more you ate of those negative-calories foods, the quicker your weight would disappear. Is the idea feasible? If it is, I would dearly like to know where the embryo derives its energy supply to undertake the metabolism necessary to transform the contents of the egg into chick. Its only outside energy input comes from the mother hen, which keeps the egg at a temperature compatible with life but does not supply any extra for metabolic purposes. If the principle did work, then you would need nothing more that a diet of two dozen eggs a day to take 2,000 calories out of your diet. Sadly, it is nonscience, not science.

Some diets claim that foods should be separated out, like the Hay diet in which three meals are eaten, each containing bread and potatoes (one meal), noodles and bread (another meal) and fruit and proteins (third meal). This is the first of the fad diets in which I know of no evidence of actual harm. However, it seems to offer little to justify it as a weight-loss regime.

There have been many other diets which are marketed for their snappy titles, rather than for any soundly-based reason; there is the 'drinking man's diet', the 'calories don't count', even a 'life without bread'. There is the F-plan diet, based on the eating of pulses, which adds to the bulk of the intestinal load and also produced a great deal of extra gas since the composition of beans is somewhat indigestible. The expulsion of gases from the rectum has given a new meaning to the 'F' in 'F-plan'. Pulses, if contaminated by fungi, can be a source of carcinogens, and the bulk they provide tends to retain many of the dietary components that would otherwise be absorbed. So the diet seems to work by filling the gut with material, and by holding back on absorption.

Foods That Are Very High in Calories

These contain more than 175 Calories per ounce so 16 oz per day would be more than most people would consume in terms of energy output. Those marked with an asterisk* are in excess of 200 Calories per ounce and are extremely rich in excess energy

Almonds	Lard*
Fat cooked bacon	Margarine*
Fried bread	Oils*
Butter*	Pastry (rich)
Peanut butter	Peanuts
Rich cakes	Peanut butter
Cashew nuts	Pork chop, fat, grilled
Cooking fat*	Ritz crackers
Clotted cream	Safflower oil*
(Crisps are 145 C per oz)	Shortbread (rich)
Buttered crumpets*	Spry cooking fat*
Dripping*	Suet*
Fried whitebait	Sunflower oil*
Flora margarine*	

Foods That Provide Negligible Energy

A list of foodstuffs which provide less than 8 Calories per ounce, and which can be eaten in moderate amounts without contributing significantly to energy intake (over 12 oz would have to be eaten to contribute 100 Calories)

Asparagus
Bean sprouts
Beans (French)
Blackberry
Broccoli
Brussels sprout
Cabbage
Carrot
Cauliflower
Celeriac
Celery
Chicory
Chives
Courgette
Cranberry
Cress
Cucumber
Endive
Garlic
Gherkin
Grapefruit
Kale
Leek
Lemon
Lettuce
Loganberry
Mandarin

Marrow
Melon
Mustard and cress
Oatmeal porridge (boiled)
Onion
Orange
Parsley
Passion fruit
Pear
Pepper (sweet)
Pumpkin
Quince
Radish
Raspberry
Saccharin
Sauerkraut
Seakale
Spinach
Strawberry
Swede
Tangerine
Tea
Tomato
Turnip
Vinegar
Watercress

Any diet which restricts calorie intake will cause weight loss which can be as much as a pound a day during the first week. This is because glycogen and other readily-available energy sources in the body are instantly mobilised for use, as a replacement for what the food is now lacking; and that with water losses causes a sudden drop in body weight for a week or so. From then on even a severely-restricted diet cannot result in a regular loss of more than, say, a couple of pounds a week. One diet has been claimed to lose 25 lb per week. To do this you would need to stop all eating, and then exercise in the Arctic for a week, 24 hours a day. It is an impossible target and a spurious claim, unless miracles are still available for the devotee.

Our attitudes to diet have developed a strange emphasis in recent years. People actually buy things to eat. Yet dieting involves what you do *not* eat, not what you *do*. I have recently read a booklet which begins by emphasising that your life may become consumed by the time it all takes. And this is the key to part of the problem – dieting is seen as a task, a problem, a hurdle. Yet the key to dieting should be the *lessening* of problems, and the removal of emphasis from huge amounts of fattening food in your life. Purchasing special foods and spending time and money on dieting can replace one form of concern and stress with another, and that is no good for anyone.

For a normal human, the level at which their weight is set is internally determined (see Chapter One) and over-eating will not cause you to become heavier if your 'adipostat' is set at a lower level. Plenty of people eat like horses, and never put on an ounce. Over-eating will not by itself make you fat. On the other hand, no matter what your weight, *under*-eating *will* make you thin. If you consume fewer calories in a day than those you expend, you are bound to lose weight. I am inclined to feel that some people do find this much easier than others, because of the setting of their internal regulatory mechanisms; but no matter how true that may be there is no possibility that you will put on fat if you are not eating enough.

The main reason why people should try to stay reasonably slim is because it is healthy. Experiments with animals have always shown that if you restrict the diet you find the animals's life expectancy goes up. It seems that this is equally true of people. On the basis of current research you might say, simply, EAT LESS, LIVE LONGER.

Calculating how much less is not so easy. It is known that the metabolic rate varies not only from person to person (fat people usually having a *higher* metabolic rate than thin ones) but that it varies in the same person from time to time, and the rate depends on the diet. Once the glycogen that is readily available has been used, the body will change its metabolic rate in order to minimise losses, and at the same time will liberate energy from the least essential parts of the body. Recent research has suggested that people burn up less than it has been popular to claim – the British Department of Health and the World Health Organisation have both insisted that the rate at which a body burns energy is 2,150 per day (women) and 2,500 a day (men). It may in fact be that the real figures are nearer 1,700 a day (women) and 2,000 (men). This is very important, for it means that a female reader of these words who was – as is very possible – rather below the average levels about which I speak might then be on a diet that is actually not causing any weight loss at all. 1,500 calories a day is a likely expenditure level for such a person, and a diet of 1,500 calories is probably what she would eat, every day, as part of a weight-loss diet. She may be aiming at 1,000 but 1,500 is more likely to be what she is really eating.

According to the conventional wisdom, this level would provide 500 calories less than her daily requirement, and since a pound of fat provides about 3,000 calories it would be a mere week before she had burned up a pound of fat. That would be a stone lost in a year. However, if her metabolic demands are actually at the lower rate, then she is eating what she needs to eat to stay as fat. She is complaining to her friends or her husband that she is below the 1,500 calorie level, and is still not losing weight. That is an exceedingly depressing prospect, particularly when people act as though they do not believe her.

The only counsel one could offer would be for her to go on a 1,000 calorie diet, and stick to it. At that rate she is bound to lose weight. Though even here I stop for thought, as research from some of the mountain people in Africa has suggested that they can exist on about this level of intake, and if so then there may yet be some people in Britain who can survive on that level without weight loss.

The only way to lose weight is to decide to eat fewer calories, and that is that. And to stick to the decision! It is vitally important to check the value of foods in terms of what they provide as energy, and for this a list of calorie contents, though helpful, need not to be consulted at every turn of the road. In most cases it is obvious what a food contains if its function is considered. Thus, there will be a range of raw materials in foods like eggs or beans, because they are the resting stage from which a new generation will emerge, so each must contain a good deal of food reserves that will nourish the emerging embryo (whether plant or animal).

It is clear that celery will contain little of that sort, since its function is to present the leaves at the top of the stalk to the light. Potatoes are a resting stage for the survival of the plant, and so must contain energy. Fats and oils all have similar energy content. Meat clearly contains amino acids that are needed to build new flesh. It is the building up of a total vision of what a food actually *is* which can do much to enable you to make snap decisions.

Here is an example of how it works in practice. You go to an Indian restaurant. Suppose you choose a creamy korma with rice, an onion bahjee and a chapati or nan. You can see the evidence of calories in the creamy sauce; the bahjee is held together with floury paste before being deep fried, and so is also rich in calories; the bread is oily and rich in calories too. The total calorific value of such a meal would be around 1,750 calories, which would enable someone to put on a scrap of weight if that was all that was eaten all day. Now take a tandoori meal: here the chicken is not cooked in an oily and creamy sauce, but in a charcoal-heated oven. No additional oil is added, and much of the fat from the meat itself melts out and runs away. Eat a little salad with it too. Have a helping of raitha (yoghurt with cucumber) and a poppadum. There is clear evidence here that you are choosing foods that are less fattening – how much lower they are in calories could be a considerable surprise, for the meal rates around 550 calories, less than one-third the previous example.

So there is no need to stop going to restaurants, or to assume that cutting your calorie intake should be equated with hardship. Slimming should never interrupt your normal life, but should amount to a change of life-style. This is also important if you wish to *stay* slim. Many people who lose weight in a diet put it all back again at Christmas, and end up as fat as they were.

Exercise is helpful, though remember that even whilst you sleep your brain is burning up about one-fifth of your total calorie turnover, and your liver is burning up a quarter of it; and the rating of the human body – about the same as a 60–watt light bulb left continuously burning – shows how efficient the body is at putting such a small amount of energy to such effective use. Far better than going on a crash diet is the life-style change I advocate.

Weigh yourself after a year should be the philosophy, and do not bother too much about changes week by week.

In the real world, nobody is able to resist the chance to monitor their own downward progress, and so people do weigh themselves. But always remember the long-term goal of a slow and steady loss until you reach a good weight for your own physique. Do not try to diet stringently if you are a good shape anyhow, for there is no point in working hard to keep yourself at a specified weight if your natural body weight would only be a few pounds heavier. Avoid the crash diet principle, for it can be dangerous; and do not expect to keep the same weight throughout your life. I have said earlier, the body changes itself in the light of the contingencies which arise, and everyone should expect a certain change in shape and weight as the years go by.

I do not care for the average height and weight tables that appear in books and magazines. The only way to know if you are over-fat is to work out, through a formula, what proportion of the body is composed of fat reserves. This can be calculated from skin-fold measurements. You can get an idea of how fat you are inside by taking a pinch of skin on the inside surface of your relaxed forearm. It should be a few millimetres, representing the skin fold itself; if it is more than that (and you can feel it easily) then your fat reserves are probably more than they need be. The sensible attitude is to look at yourself, without any clothes, in a mirror. Be critical. Or compare holiday photographs and see how you have looked over the years. It is the personal appearance that gives away an overweight problem at a glance, and not mathematical formulae.

The danger inherent in the tables I mentioned is their inevitable variation. People are not all the same, and the tables have flexibility which can upset their reliability. One example shows the weights given as 'plus or minus 5 lb'. It gives the weight for a given height as 10st 1 lb, within the nearest ten pounds. But consider what that implies. The person who should be 10st 1 lb on average could be ten pounds light; and you must add to that the ±5 lb factor. So this person could have a weight of 15lb less, and weigh 8st 13lb and still be in the virtually 'normal' category. This also works in reverse, so you can *add* ten pounds to the target weight of 10 st 1 lb, which gives 10 st 11 lb; and then add the extra 5 lb making 11 st 1 lb altogether.

This means that the table could show a person of 8 st 13 lb

fitting well onto the table as 'within the normal limits' when they should really be (at the top end of the same scale) 11st 11 lb. So a person could be an astonishing 30 lbs overweight, and still derive security from the tables that they were really about right.

Personal dimensions vary so much, that the only sensible way to assess your weight and height ratio is to look at yourself in the mirror. Scientific data about average weights are helpful if interpreted sensibly, but they can give a spurious authority to a result that is otherwise unacceptable.

Once you have decided to restrict calories in your diet, comes the question, *which* calories? One easy answer is the excess calories in sugar or breadsticks – things one can simply *avoid*. Another comes from avoiding the easily recognised calorific foods: excess cream, butter and margarine, sweets and cakes, endless crisps and peanuts. But there then arises the possibility, not merely of dietary reduction, but of dietary change. One excellent way to make a safer diet is to cut out a good deal of saturated fats. This is for several reasons. One of them is that fats are the most concentrated form of energy (remember that a pound is equivalent to 3,000 calories). Another is that saturated fats in large amounts are foreign to our bodies, and on that basis we might well do without so many. The third is that they may be involved with the incidence of coronary heart disease. This is *not* a matter of proven fact, as we shall see shortly, but it has enough in it to make the precaution sensible. Changing to unsaturated fats seems to offer some chance of improving one's health, though as we have seen rancid fats (and unsaturated fats stand a good chance of undergoing this form of deterioration) pose problems in themselves.

Stressed vegetables (notably stressed celery) and rancid fatty substances and rancid oils should be avoided, as should mouldy pulses and stale peanuts. Here too there is no evidence to prove that carcinogens or mutagens in these foods ever survive long enough to alter the genetic complement of our cells to cause a harmful lesion, and it may be that our well-documented anti-cancer mechanisms are in themselves enough protection to resist all this. But such foods can be avoided, and if they are rich in potentially harmful molecules it would make good sense to cut them out.

Additional fibre, through eating fruit and vegetables, will clearly assist the proper functioning of the digestive process and may have more profound effects on an improved state of health. And if

144

you wish to take a dietary supplement – zinc, say, vitamin C, multivitamin tablets – there is no reason why this should not be sensible, even though most diets provide more than enough of the vitamins and minerals we basically require.

And change your way of cooking for a less fatty, lower calorie equivalent. Poach eggs, rather than fry them. Eat toast in place of fried bread. Don't soak baked potatoes in butter. Read labels, and avoid foods that contain unnecessary additives or hidden salt or sugar. Eat less food. Rather than sit in front of the TV, eating a take-away meal, prepare food that is deliciously tasty, healthy, fun to eat. Do not imagine that convenience foods are there for your convenience, and just that. By being over-convenient they prevent you from having control over what you eat, and can remove one of the great sources of family pleasure and social communion in the home. You eat quickly, watching the TV, and then do little else. The cycle of sitting in traffic jams, sitting in offices, sitting in front of the TV, is one which economic hardship has tended to inflict on women as much as men, and the fact that it is labelled 'liberation' should not be such a successful exercise in propaganda as to blind us to what has truly happened. Take control of your diet. Prepare food you like to eat, and the need to eat it to excess begins to wane. That is why the primitive societies in the world, which should be so deprived, are in fact so close knit, so content, and, so far as diet goes, so healthy.

You will note that I am not subscribing to the view that fat causes heart attacks, for I do not believe it is as simple as that. I do not believe that plant fibre in the diet is the leading factor, nor that it is sugar. Take the 'fat' argument. Firstly, there are other well-known factors involved. Cigarette smoking, which can be active (as in the case of smokers), or passive (as in the case of people who sit next to them) increases the likelihood of coronary heart disease. Patients with high blood pressure run a far greater risk of suffering heart disease than does the rest of society. It is not always true that a reduction in cholesterol in the diet produces a lessening of the chances of suffering a heart attack. One example is a community is found in Roseto, Pennsylvania. Of the town's 1,630 inhabitants over 90% had descended from the same small Italian immigrant community. They ate just as much of the greasy and rich foods as they could, rich in lard, gravy and dripping.

Over a six-year period of study none of those aged under 47 died of a coronary heart attack, whilst amongst the older men in the community the death rate from coronary artery disease was around half that typical of the surrounding population. Meanwhile, members of the group that left the community to settle elsewhere featured levels of disease that compared with the rest of the American population. Diet was not the main factor here.

What of plant fibre in the diet? The eskimos traditionally ate a diet which contained no plant matter at all, indeed the eskimo populations did not know what a plant looked, let alone tasted, like. They subsisted on fish and meat throughout the year. Clearly, plant fibre in the diet is not vital for human health either, for in spite of that lack they remained a vigorously healthy people.

Is sugar the answer? Levels of sugar consumption are often compared with those of coronary heart disease, but many of those figures could be pure coincidence. One of the examples that suggests sugar is not implicated, lies in the Caribbean. There the black populations eat a diet which is by tradition rich in sugary additives (sugarcane is an important item of diet). Yet coronary heart disease is uncommon amongst those people.

There is, though, a further common denominator which is not sufficiently taken into consideration, and that is the question of life-style and our fitness for the lives that we are obliged to lead. It is the life-style factor which is particularly important, I conclude. The Italians in Pennsylvania, the Eskimo people in the Arctic wastes, the ebullient blacks in Jamaica, like the oft-quoted examples of primitive peoples living in deserts, or up mountains, sometimes eating herbs, perhaps subsisting on buried beetles or tree-bark; they are communities that live in a communicative world where problems are faced and where life presents dramatic problems that they themselves handle. Our own communities delegate such responsibilities to anonymous professionals. Experts take decisions on our behalf. That is why there is a good correlation between colour TV sets and the incidence of coronary heart disease (a correlation that is better than the one that exists between sugar and coronary artery disease). It is not that TV 'causes' heart attacks. It is that our lives in modern communities subjugate us to such an extent that our individuality and our personal freedom to influence destiny are limited. Energy-rich compounds that are liberated into the bloodstream in order to tackle problems are left there, unused, as we sit and mutely endure our lot; hence the so-called 'furring up' of the arteries.

For example, there is a well-known study that has shown how

bus drivers are more liable to ill-health than bus conductors. this proves, says the conclusion, that exercise is the important factor which gives the conductors their improved state of health. I question that, for even though this may be the correct conclusion there is no evidence it must be so. Parallel causality may also be at work here, for it could be that the driver reacts to the frustrations of his work, whilst the conductor is enjoying interpersonal contact and has a chance to control their relationships with people on the bus on a scale that outstrips the driver, wrestling with other drivers with whom he has no personal contact at all.

This is not to say that parallel causality works in every case; it may yet turn out that exercise is an important factor in the example I have quoted. However, the point to which I wish to direct attention is the dangerous fact that we assume too readily that the handy or convenient solution must be the right one. Often, 'right' means 'fashionable' and at the present time we look to dietary restriction and a lack of exercise as a matter of trendiness. The personal, social, psychological relationships are suffering a low profile at the present time. Yet I believe it is these factors that matter at least as much as diet in managing our health.

Taking control of one's self, one's diet, one's physical state and shape can be a start. A low-calorie diet will control weight gain if this is more than you feel is appropriate. A diet low in fat, sugar and salt, yet high in fibre, has much to be said for it, and may even have positive effects on areas of your health that you would not at first hearing associate with foodstuffs at all – but in many cases these relationships remain tenuous or unproven.

But 'suffering' a diet, feeling 'forced' to adopt it, this is not the makings of a healthy life-style. It is the quest for freedom, for personal relaxation and individual expression, for meaningfully enjoyable relationships within the family, and for the establishment of close contact between parents and children, that provides the most convincing future answer to many of these difficulties. And I have no doubt that the making of good meals and the enjoyment of an actively intimate family circle, or a group of loving friends, matter more than the latest fad diet.

We may argue about the relative importance of additives, fats and sugars. But there can be no sensible doubt that our life-style is often stressful and inflexible. And, whatever may be said about our food, that most surely can disrupt life, and even end it. Taken in its broader context, the changes I have put forward could influence every aspect of personal harmony. The diet will be just the beginning.

INDEX